Writing in the Cegeps: an anthology of new fiction

ACKNOWLEDGEMENTS

First, to all of the contributors to this anthology who convey their love of literature to students and who also work at the craft of writing; your faith in this project and your talent and passion made the labour all worthwhile. To all of our students, past, present, and future, it is to give to you the gift that the power to tell is glorious that these stories have been crafted. Thanks also to my colleagues in the English Department of Marianopolis College for their interest, support, and enthusiasm for this undertaking. A special thanks to Charlene Milne for her meticulous care in preparing this manuscript. Above all, to Zach, whose passion for writing always fuels my own, and to Suzanne, whose love and support have always been the building blocks of my dreams.

The editor wishes to acknowledge the following publications where some of these stories first appeared: Barry Webster's story "Sweat" first appeared in a slightly different form in *Maisonneuve Magazine*. Harold Hoefle's "Down Time" was first published in *Exile*. Zsolt Alapi's "Eva" first appeared in *Front & Centre* and subsequently as part of a chapbook, "Three Stories" (Mercutio Press, Montréal).

Writing in the Cegeps: an anthology of new fiction

edited by

Z s o l t   A l a p i

To Steve,
Fellow writer.
Thanks for your
support,

[signature]

SIREN SONG

Cover design: David Drummond
Printed by Marquis Book Printing Inc.

Copyright © Zsolt Alapi 2008

Dépot legal, Bibliothèque et Archives nationales du Québec and the Library and Archives Canada, 2008
All rights reserved.

LIBRARY AND ARCHIVES CANADA CATALOUGING IN PUBLICATION

Writing in the Cegeps: an anthology of new fiction/Zsolt Alapi, editor.

ISBN 978-0-9783455-1-8 (pbk.)

1. Short stories, Canadian (English). 2. Canadian fiction (English)—Québec (Province). 3. Canadian fiction (English)—21st century.
I. Alapi, Zsolt, 1950-

PS8329.1.W74 2008   C813.0108353   C2008-903057-5

Published by:

Siren Song Publishing
2331 Beaconsfield Avenue
Montréal, Québec H4A 2G9

www.sirensongpublishing.com

Printed in Canada on 100% post-consumer recycled paper

For Suzanne and Zach

SIREN SONG

FORWARD

The English departments of universities and colleges have professed a love for literature and the word, claiming to pass along this passion through teaching. Sadly and all too often, what passes as teaching is critical interpretation that is more centered on a methodology or philosophy than on the actual exploration of the creative process. Now that the pundits and critics have declared the Author as Dead and the text as nothing but verbal pleasuring, a sound and fury signifying only the signifier, how can students be taught at all to appreciate the simplest yet most fundamental of acts: the telling of a tale?

Goethe spoke of "Dichtung und Wahrheit" — poetry and truth, and fortunately there are still writers out there writing for the human ear "given to write…," as Robert Creeley once said. These are the writers for whom the act is one of inspiration, and, dare I say it, love of the vagaries of being human while believing in a fundamental truth found in our varied experiences. It is these writers who you will encounter throughout these pages in voices that are alternately angry, envious, desirous, forlorn, etc., but, above all, longing to connect.

This anthology is the result of a shared belief on the part of those who teach literature as a labour of love, a belief resting on the faith that stories are magical *because* they convey a profound human truth, and that a writer bears testament to this — "man standing by his word," as Charles Olson wrote. So this book came about, first, to showcase the talent of those who teach in the Cegeps, and second to provide a collection of new fiction that connects to the lives of those they teach and to the lives of anyone with a passion for reading.

Finally, this book is dedicated to all of those who teach *and* write and who believed in this project to bring to our students and to readers alike stories that come from the very heart of life. W.C. Williams once stated: "No ideas, but in things." By this he meant to end the Cartesian trap that posits reason above emotion and analysis and intellectualizing above direct experience. For those who have ever felt moved by a tale well-wrought, felt the pleasure of a well-turned phrase, or the shock and startle of our humanity and its ability to move us to love and to horror, it is for your true ear that these stories have been crafted. The "things" that constitute these stories are no less than the very things that make us so perplexingly human.

Enjoy the journey.

Zsolt Alapi
Montréal
June 2008

CONTENTS

Glory

Tanya Bellehumeur-Allatt

Glory

The gold tooth shimmers inside Florida's mouth. She knows it. Even when her mouth is shut and her body is sleeping, the tooth is shimmering in the darkness, declaring the glory of God. It is Florida's greatest treasure, and she proudly displays it for photographers with flash cameras, skeptical conservatives, excited schoolchildren. She keeps a flashlight in her purse so that she can illuminate her mouth at any time: in the subway, on the assembly line, in the cafeteria. Anytime someone asks to see, she opens wide and shows them the glory.

"Got it at church. Just came down out of the sky and into my mouth."

And everyone who knows her knows it's true. Florida Simms' front left tooth was rotten for most of her life. It was gray with black splotches right there in the middle of her smile, and ugly. Florida's been poor as dirt all her life, never even touched real gold till now.

"I was in this church service, and we was cheering you know, like Roberta cheers when the Cubs hit a home run on TV, and there were two thousand of us and we were jumpin' and cheerin' and doing the wave for Jesus and then there was a hush that fell over us and we was all a-swayin' and fallin' to our kneeses and some was weepin' and then I heared someone, real excited like, say 'Gold dust! There's gold dust on my Bible!' And I turned to Roberta, and her hair was all gold like with dust. She looked like a fairy with it twinkling through and catching the light and I started laughin' to think that Jesus was makin' Roberta a princess and Roberta just looks at me with eyes round as saucers and she say, 'Lookit! Lookit!' And she start grabbin' people round her and she pointin' at my mouth and starin', and laughin' and cryin' and Mama Richards she give me the mirror from her eyeshadow compact and when I sees it I yell 'Glory! Glory! God done visited me in my mouth!'

"And the next day me and Roberta and Mama Richards take the bus to 15th avenue and Cranmore and we sees the dentist there on the 5th floor and he say to me he ain't ever seen such a fine gold tooth as this one here in my mouth. And he look at me all funny like, and he take down my name and the name of the church and he look again at that tooth under his fancy mirror for a long, long time, rubbin' his forehead. He look so long and hard at that tooth it was like he was memorizin' it or waitin' for it to disappear or tell him somthin'.

'That's a beautiful tooth. That's some tooth.' That's what Mr. Dentist say over and over again.

"And I tell him, 'Almighty God put it there. That there tooth comes from Heaven. And Jesus loves you and he has a plan for your life, Mr. Dentist.'

"And I wink at him, and he give me a toothbrush from his drawer and a little white package of cinnamon flavour floss and I say 'Thank you very much' and put 'em in my handbag before he change his mind, 'cause people jus' don' give things away for free anymore, you know.

"And at the produce stall on Mackinnon I smile real wide for Ole Man Johnson, and he jus' shake his head behind the cabbages all piled up, and I know he already heared about it from the guys at the bowling alley, 'cause stuff like this spreads like a house on fire. It ain't every day you meet someone with the glory of God, the real glory of God, in her mouth."

House on Fire

Mara Gutmanis Grey

House on Fire

"What are you doing," he said. "You'll set the house on fire. Give me that." He grabbed the dishrag from her, let it drop on the stove extinguishing the flame that had shot up from the fat in the pan in which she had been about to fry his fish. Now she stood framed in the kitchen doorway looking blank as she watched him, wondering what he had done differently from what she had intended to do. He turned to her and pushed the smouldering rag into the crook of her elbow giving her a disapproving look. She started, about to protest, but he had already walked away.

She bit her lip and moved week-kneed to the counter and began chopping the onion. Her mascara stained tears plopped on the cutting board as she lopped off a sliver of her finger and couldn't find it anywhere at all. Smarting, she blinked several times. She heard him switch on the evening news. She saw him entrenched behind his crossword. Blindly, she dropped the chopped bits into the sputtering hot pan. A few drops seared her flesh. Her body winced like the flanks of a horse bitten by a gnat. As she drained the potatoes, hot steam veiled the kitchen window. Her nostrils flared; she half sighed half moaned as she watched a rosette spreading on the white of the potatoes. Reaching across the counter, she grabbed a Kleenex to tie around her finger. She went on to set the table. The gesture was as familiar as breathing. It hadn't always been this way.

Once running through a field, the light flashing through the trees, he had run after her, laughing, caught her by the leg, dragged her to the grass, made her feel the sun bursting in her womb, till the mosquitoes forced them apart.

She went to the sink, opened the tap, let the water wash away the drops of blood, turned to the stove, flicked on the gas. The flame shot up. She turned it off, then on again, without a flame this time. She craned her head, listening for the barely audible seeping. She called him for supper. He came with the newspaper under his arm. Without looking at her, he unfolded the paper and began to read. As soon as she had served him, he began to chew; his eyes always on the headlines. She took off her apron, and walking by him announced she had to go. He glanced up at her, didn't see her dark pupil tunnelling into the distance as she turned the corner and left the kitchen. With half a grimace, he went back to the paper and his fish.

She went upstairs, changed into a pale blue dress, screwed in her gold hoops, loosened the greying hair that had clung shapelessly to her skull for so long, outlined her trembling lips with a crimson lipstick she had used the last time he had taken her out, caught her beckoning reflection in the glass and, beyond that, the laced branches of the elm outside swaying in the wind. She picked up her bag and walked downstairs, past the kitchen where her husband sat, and out into the dark night, leaving behind a house on fire.

Who's Going to Believe You?

Lawrence L. Szigeti

Who's Going to Believe You?

"Omid Emami!"

He stirred at the calling out of something like his name. What next?

The hard wooden bench on which he lay hurt his back, his left, and his right side — hc could turn no more to find even a semblance of comfort. He hadn't been able to fall asleep for hours. Though the light was on all the time, it was more the shuffling, clinking, swearing, and the unseemly orders balked out intermittently, yet at regular enough intervals, that thwarted all attempts at lulling himself to sleep. The *human* factor, *quoi*.

"Venez-venez! On vous transfère!"

There was no point in asking where, or why — they wouldn't say anyway. One of the first things he noticed in his new legal state was that he *deserved* no information on what and why and when things were happening to him.

Once outside the cell, he was paired with a silent, equally downcast, and utterly innocuous looking guy with a beard and with the same type of dazed, incomprehensive look in his eyes. Handcuffed to one another, they were both shoved into a waiting transfer vehicle. There they sat until the officers rounded up the rest of the night's catch: a still half-stoned drunkard, a tattooed, muscular blond guy with raw pent-up masculine energy, a half-naked youngster cursing in Spanish, two hookers, an older and a totally stoned younger one, and half a dozen others. Apart from the women, who were in the front half of the back of the truck, separated by bars as in a cage, all the others were packed into a small space, so that they all felt like herded cattle, gulping for air.

At least half an hour passed before the truck was started up and finally cleared the gates. Through a tiny round window in the back he could see that it was a wonderful, sunny day, with blue skies. He kept his eyes fixed on the round window, his only contact with the outside world, with normalcy, with things so far taken for granted: sunshine, free-moving traffic, trees, people on the streets going about their business.

Now he could only see in patches the tree branches overarching the street on which they were driven, whirled walk up wrought iron stairs so typical of the city, and some of the landmark skyscrapers that bobbed up as the road undulated through the wave-like urban topography.

Suddenly they came to a halt. The vehicle manoeuvred into a parking position, the officers got out. He could see them walking across to an Italian bar. He tried to guess where they were, but this was the downtown area, and he rarely had the opportunity to make it down here. Apart from the first two weeks after his arrival some five years ago now, he had been working like a mule — and he counted himself lucky for it.

"Peel Street."

The ordinary looking guy to his left, the one he was handcuffed to, offered the name up, something like a reassurance, like a mantra destined to give them the feeling that they were still anchored in the real world. Dangling, as if at the very end of a rope, very near the end of their tether, but still hanging in.

The officers, joking loudly, dawdled back to the truck munching on doughnuts and clutching steaming cups of coffee. They started the engine up, and the truck pulled away with a jerk that made them grab onto each other lest they all pile up on the floor as freshly slaughtered carcasses on their way to the meat processing plant.

"I just didn't see it coming."

The guy next to him muttered the words more to himself, not really in an effort to communicate — yet he understood it all too well. The words could have been his.

"Why didn't I see it coming? It had been this cat and mouse game throughout the whole month! And to think of having given up my job, moved half way across the country, hatched this neat little idea to make ends meet for all of us, promising to get rid of all those debts raked up by mindless spending..."

He had the sensation of some echo in his mind. Indeed, all work, no play for four years in order to have the money for a comfortable three and a half with a fancy living room, matching furniture, fully equipped kitchen, and cable —– plus the debilitating one-way air ticket, the thousands of dollars for all the paperwork, the sponsorship, the matchmakers and middlemen, the intricate deals within the community here and back home... All the high hopes for a new life with an educated, articulate, modern home-builder, someone who would complement him perfectly, whom he could be proud of, whom he would pamper, look up to, care for — someone arranged for him following timeless custom.

"Hysterical name-calling, that's what it was. No, it wasn't pretty. But by the time the patrol car squeaked to a stop next to us, we were holding hands and on our way to making up. Still, they instantly separated us, and having talked to each of us alone, booked me on a charge of *voie de fait*. And while I admitted having quarrelled, all they actually saw was people in an embrace..."

It all came flooding back. Getting home after the long shift to another supper of bread and sardines, the third in a row. He just couldn't let it pass. He risked being made fun of for not asserting his rights. Since they got together, there had not been the slightest attempt at having a hot meal prepared, as was the ancient rule. The fact that there were strictly no conjugal services either from the very start, he didn't even dare mention. He would instead fiddle about it to his friends.

"They told me they had a signed deposition against me, and that I'd better think of returning to my home province, for we'll be barred from ever seeing each other again. So much for promises of a fresh start together..."

Ditto here, he thought. Except, he was probably not going to be allowed back into his own apartment, and would have to find shelter with friends. He might even be deported, who knows? Worst of all, all his savings were back in there too. With hindsight, he knew it was foolish to have blown his top. He had been here long enough to know that it would be held against him. Indeed, one little call to the police, and he was done for. He was nowhere near as articulate, educated, and innocent sounding. When the cops came, they didn't even bother asking about *his* version of the facts, but even if they had, he spoke little English, and absolutely no French. The last words in their native tongue, in response to his utter indignation, were still ringing in his ears.

The transfer truck had suddenly stopped, turned around, and reversed into a building. The early morning ride through the picturesque town had come to an end. After a few start-go, start-go attempts, they docked. The gates came crushing down. They were *secured*.

Laughing Lazarus

Tom Abray

Laughing Lazarus

Howard Reid was living on rue de l'Esplanade then, just north of Bernard. He had a four-and-a-half on the second floor with a little kitten named Rice. His place was being renovated, but he and Rice stayed throughout the ordeal. The ceiling was being rebuilt, walls were being moved. This was all because of an accident that had occurred a few months before. One weekend when the landlord was away the hot water heater had exploded and its contents seeped through the floor, turning Howard's ceilings to mush and drawing long stalactite stains on his walls.

One night when I was out for a walk, I stopped by unannounced. Through the window I saw Rice run to the door, meow, then twist back and meow again. Howard undid the lock and welcomed me into the foyer. His curly brown hair was tied in a ponytail. He wore his corduroy shirt untucked, which accentuated his slight pot-belly. Looking past him, I could see workhorses and strips of transparent plastic sheeting, a futile attempt to limit the spread of gypsum dust.

We left Rice to amuse himself and walked across the street toward Café Romolo. I noticed Howard reaching for his pockets. He snapped his fingers regretfully.

"Forget something?"

"Damn. Wallet."

"I'll treat you. But you have to tell me a story."

"Oh, Michel," he chuckled, shaking his head. "That's easy."

My name is Michael, but Howard once called me "Meeshel" years ago and it has stuck ever since.

"What is it this time?" I asked.

"Do you remember Laura?" he asked. "The girl from Whitehorse I met at Winnie's."

"No sex, right?"

Howard laughed.

Sex. They had considered it — as I recalled — at four, perhaps five in the morning, but that was all. There was "nothing physical" that night, and the next day Laura had to catch a bus. They agreed to write, but Howard's lease was almost up. He didn't know where he was moving, so he gave out his mother's address. She could forward him any letters once he re-settled. She did. And Howard always meant to write back.

We ordered two mint teas and after the waitress left, Howard shook his head with amazement. "How, how," he asked, "how do I do it, Michel?

"I take it you've heard from her."

"No! That would be too simple. I heard from my mom. Last week."

"Oh, mama's in this one."

"She's one of the main characters, Michel. Just you wait!"

She wasn't mama, though. She was 'mum', born and raised within sight of the English Channel, married in Toronto, widowed in Oshawa, when Howard was twelve.

"And what did Mom want?" I asked.

"To send me a letter." He said "letter" as though it were significant.

"She wrote you a letter?"

"No." I'd used up one of my free guesses.

"Laura wrote you a letter?"

He shook his head. No, no, no: my imagination was no match for his life. He had to tell me: "Laura wrote Mum a letter."

"Ah!"

He was smiling smugly, delighting in the next part.

"I'll ask," I said. "Why did she write your mother?"

"To discuss my funeral, of course."

"Oh, is she planning it?" I said cleverly.

"No. She *attended* it."

"Did she? And how was it?"

"You're keeping up, Michel." He chuckled for a moment and then shook his head. "Ah, it was beautiful from what I hear."

Our tea arrived. The waitress asked if we wanted to pay on the spot or run a tab. We paid. After all, I had just shown up unannounced on a weekday. This wouldn't be one of those all-nighters we used to have. That phase had ended badly for Howard — a broken heart over a waitress with curls. He still felt a lingering pain when the weather was damp.

"Where was I?"

"You're dead," I said as I lowered the teabag into the little chrome pot.

"Dearly departed."

"So? What the hell happened?"

"Where do I begin?"

Like many people born under an unlucky star, he was a good storyteller and he knew it. He fiddled with his tea cup to let the suspense accumulate, and then, with a stage chuckle, he began.

"Laura was taking the bus across Canada again. No, wait. My mother called last week all 'Howard Anthony, what's going on? Blah, blah, blah.' I couldn't understand. She was going here, she was going there. I said, 'Mum, slow down, first things first.' So she told me she got this letter addressed to Mrs. Reid, but you know she doesn't go by Reid because after my dad died she switched back to West. But she opened it anyway and I said, 'Mum, that's a federal offence to open mail that doesn't belong to you.' She was almost crying. I said, 'Mum, what's really the matter?'"

In the letter Laura explained how she'd met Howard in Montreal, how, even though they'd only spent eight hours together, he'd affected her deeply. Her tone was respectful. She wrote "the meeting", not "the evening", and the glowing description of Howard's character made him sound like a modern saint. Something had to be wrong.

Even though she hadn't seen Howard since then, Laura wrote, she thought of him often. In fact, she'd been thinking of him the same day she noticed his obituary in the Toronto Star. It was quite a coincidence. She was travelling across Canada by bus to visit family in P.E.I. There was a short stopover in Toronto and she flipped through the paper while eating lunch. The obituary "struck her to the heart". She saw that the funeral would be held the next day — in Oshawa, of course — so she went straight to the counter to change her ticket.

She was pleased to see so many people paying their respects. She wanted to come over and talk to Mrs Reid, but, well, she had not. So now she was writing this — so Howard's mother would know what an impression her son had made on someone else's life, even someone who had only met him once. (But even from the one, brief meeting she could tell Howard was a special person.)

"So she actually thought she went to your funeral?"

Howard was sipping his tea, letting me absorb the tale. His eyes grew wide and he pulled a mischievous expression. He should've been an actor. "Thinks," he said.

"She doesn't know yet?!"

He couldn't help but laugh. "No," he said. "I just got the letter yesterday. There's a phone number on it. I'm going to phone her."

"My God, that's going to be something. You'll scare the crap out of her."

"I know. I'm a little afraid. I have to figure out how to explain very quickly, before she faints or has a heart attack."

As we sipped our tea, I thought of Howard's best head-shaking moments, like the recent one about a girl he met in a café. They chatted over coffee and then he boldly walked her home. Afterward, happening upon a flower shop, he bought her a dozen roses, rushed back to her apartment and mistakenly presented the bouquet to her roommate.

Or the time he borrowed $200 from a guy who turned out to be a mobster. Or when he unknowingly bought a stolen car; or took the same course twice at university, or was accidentally administered an urethral swab. The list went on. But this latest ... it had to be the best, or worst yet.

"Your poor mom," I said. "There must have been half a second when she thought you'd died and she'd missed the funeral."

His hands flew up in the air. "She's much more worried about Laura!" Slipping into Mum's voice he said, "'Howard Anthony, what did you do to that girl? Here's the number. I want you to phone her right away and put an end to her grief, the poor thing.'"

"Ah!" I'd caught him out. "So you've actually had the number since last week?"

He tried to distract me from his blushing with a laugh.

"But you have to do it some time," I said.

"I know." He looked around the room and then bit down on his favourite fingernail. "But it feels kind of *good* to be dead."

"Sure: you're missed."

"And I was *mourned*, Michel."

"Too bad you weren't there."

"That'd be too weird."

"How'd you die anyway?"

"I don't know. I'm afraid to ask."

We finished our tea and I walked him home. The air was cool. I heard the rattle of leaves beneath our feet. We spoke briefly of money and work. When Howard unlocked the door, Rice started to do ecstatic figure-eights around his legs. "Love!" said Howard, picking up the kitten with one hand and kissing his furry cheeks.

"I'll leave you two alone," I said.

A few blocks away I had an apartment similar to Howard's, just a little smaller but with no drywall dust, and no cat. I walked slowly, musing over Howard's "death". Suddenly, I thought of something that filled me with hope and envy. The next time the weather was damp and Howard felt that old, heavy heart-ache coming on, all he'd have to do was dial a number in Whitehorse, say his name, and with a woman's startled gasp suddenly be drawn back from the land of the dead.

Spectres

Helen Siourbas

Spectres

It ended with spectres. Between the trees, human mist, solid as smoke, closed doors. The moon was in collusion. Lina felt the betrayal as raindrops turning to ice on her skin. When it had begun, she could not say.

The maiden returned. She stepped out from behind the white trunk of a birch, pale skin shining brightly behind layers and layers of leaves. Her face mirrored the fine lines on Lina's; only the young woman's eyebrows revealed her innocence.

"Why are they following me?" Lina asked, hair still humid, frightened less by the reflection of her past self than by the insubstantial. In the distance, by the mound, she watched five spectres approaching, pentangle.

"Why are you surprised?" the maiden responded. "They are your unborn children."

*

Under the outcropping, water fell evenly, like sheets of cool fabric that reveal by concealing. Lina liked coming here at sunset, when most were eating and she could bathe in private. Her robe hung over a branch, a violet vine adding colour to the red and orange leaves of the maple. It was late in the season to be washing outdoors, but she needed to be permanently cleansed; the hot springs, salty, kept too much too close. The wind brought spiralling seeds into her hair, and Faen.

He said, "I buried them," keeping his back to her. She watched as mist dampened his shirt against his shoulder blades. She stepped over pebbles and wrapped herself in linen the colour of sky.

"Thank you."

He faced her, as she knew he would, as she hoped he wouldn't. The sound of water cascading was not quite loud enough to drown conversation, the pool not quite chill enough to freeze memory. She tied her belt into a loose knot, slipped on her sandals.

Faen's hand reached out as though he had never touched her before; he hadn't, since the maiden first ran her staff along Lina's belly as though drawing runes in the dirt.

Lina asked, "Did anything happen?"

He looked away, at the centre of the pool, where fish gathered.

"What?"

He looked back at her, his eyes reflecting the surface of the water. "I didn't see anything, but after I got up and turned away, I heard the stars fall."

*

Lina would not touch the maiden, so she pitched her voice in the range of spells. "I didn't have an abortion."

The maiden raised her staff, eyes fixed ahead on the mist. "You are thinking past instead of future. Your thoughts killed them. You didn't want them, so now you can't have them."

Lina remembered Faen's stars.

The maiden whirled, her staff striking Lina's side. Belatedly, Lina shielded her abdomen with splayed fingers. The visceral reaction, muscles contracting in a spasm that made her wince, she could not control.

"Did I tell you to bury?" the maiden cried out. "I told you to burn."

Lina remembered the sleep, the light, the dreamless twilight from which she had awakened less, because of the maiden. "You didn't say anything," she whispered. "Nothing at all."

"The ground is for growth." The maiden's hair, dark, wild, caught the moonlight. "There can be no more growth in you, neither for life nor for death. I told you to burn."

*

"Did you wish?" Lina asked Faen, her eyes turning up to the first planets of the night.

"It wasn't that kind of star fall," he said, running a finger along her cheek, her wet hair. "They were like comets blazing."

She enjoyed the ridges of his warm skin. This was how he touched her now, tentatively, as though expecting her collapse or the drop of tears. He always watched her eyes, her pupils, every dilation a possible sign. She gripped his hand with the new-found strength in her arms.

"I'm fine," she whispered.

"Except when I make you laugh."

"That was just the next day," she said, but her voice betrayed her uncertainty, her fear, her forced control. He saw it, and she felt compelled to respond:

"When will I be able to do everything I want to do? I can't even let myself laugh aloud or too deeply. I can finally bathe but can't swim across the lake. I can walk but not run. I am half my self. The rest of me is who I was before the maiden marked me."

Faen said nothing, but Lina felt the moisture at his eyes as he pressed into her, touching only her upper body.

When she screamed, it was not out of pain or frustration. Rising from the water, stepping forward from under the waterfall, a pale mist emerged in human form.

*

"But the water is my element," Lina told the maiden, glancing over her shoulder at hidden shadows. "Fire is antithetical to me."

"I saved your life," the maiden said, "yet you rebel. There is nothing more I can do for you."

"You can't just cut me off like you cut me open!" Lina's chest constricted and her breath came in gasps. *Not again,* she thought, her gaze blurring and seeking the ground, her temples pressing within. "You told me I would always have to live with this wound, but you don't tell me how to live with it. When will I have my life back?"

The maiden clasped her hands before her breast, tilted her chin down. "It is over," she said, and returned to mist.

Lina fell to her knees. She grabbed the base of her throat, trying to control the retching that robbed her of air and sent needles into her abdomen. *This will pass,* she told herself. *Why should it?* she quickly added. *Nothing else will.*

"Look up." Faen's voice guided her gaze to the safety of the sky. His hand rested between her shoulder blades, massaging the spasms away. When her breath returned, she noticed that the maiden mist had disappeared.

*

In the end, she left him by a willow tree to build a fire. She would run.

The ground was damp from the evening mist. She kept looking back, squinting, with her palms flat against her abdomen. She had heard about the bell. After earth and water and fire had failed her, she believed the wind would solve all problems. Only the breeze had yet to undermine her, unless through the maiden's words.

The bell was well-hidden, among twisted vines that reached towards the moon. Lina smiled up at it as her hand found ceramic. It was smooth and blue, laced with golden birds, though the wood of the handle was split down the centre. Lina held it up, turning to face the shades, and started to sound it vigorously.

They paused. The nearby bushes no longer shook with secrets spilling forth. Lina continued to pound clear notes, hoping with each one to see the backward motion of leaves or puffs of mist rising into the sky, before being torn apart by gales. She swung again, with a cry. The ceramic shattered, leaving her shaking a soundless stem. The shadows emerged from behind rocks and brambles.

She faced them, her breath gone, her words dry, her skin cold and damp. She began to recognize them now, familiar features and hands cupped before their waists. Through their fingers seeped blood.

Lina looked down to the pool forming beneath her, feeding the earth. She sobbed, once, and slunk to her knees, supporting herself with her hands, bloody and covered in porcelain shards.

They surrounded her slowly, each moving at a different cadence. Lina thought she heard their voices whispering fear.

"I want to be free," she said. "I want to live my life as it was, not worrying every day about what I have lost."

"What have you gained?" they asked her, one voice, layered, and Lina realized that they were of air, that the bell called to them, that every time she spoke and breathed, they would be there. Lina exhaled what breath was left stagnating in her lungs.

"How will you live?" They splayed their fingers to reveal runes carved in flesh.

Lina, surrounded by a pool of blood, warm and bright red, slightly viscous, brought her fingers to her own belly and was surprised to find it wet. She pulled away the fabric of her robe to trace the seeping scar. Beneath her touch, it burned, and as she inhaled with the pain, a wraith sublimated into vapour and flowed into her raw flesh. Lina breathed in again, removing her fingers from the path. With each breath, she absorbed a shade. When she was done, she lay on the damp ground and fell asleep.

*

Faen found her in fabric splotched red from collar to hem. He knelt beside her, touched her shoulder gently, her eyebrow, the bone at her hip. He saw her breath rise and fall in the diffuse light of dawn.

She smiled before opening her eyes, clasping his hand in hers and guiding his palm to the slow curve of her belly. His hand was warm; his touch reminded her of the time before the maiden.

"She came to me," Lina said, eyes reddish in their brown. "I saw the crone."

Faen cupped her cheek. With his other hand, he took the hem of her robe between two fingers.

"The shades could have taken me with them, but they joined in me, instead." She smiled a smile Faen had not seen in over a year. "Follow me."

She guided him back to the lake, hand in hand, where sunlight dappled the water. She waded in, her robe billowing about her in a rose cloud.

"Come." She slipped beneath the surface, emerging with hair soaked at odd angles. A leaf flew off a nearby tree and settled in her palm.

He joined her in the water, in the morning sun, wind cool on his damp cheeks, toes enmeshed in mud. Together they dove, joining the shadows beneath the waters.

It had begun with a sharp pain on a moonless night, with tears and a hollow heart.

Row by Row

Monique Polak

Row by Row

Twenty-two flats of marigolds. Twenty-two flats of purple lobelia
— not the trailing sort, though that reminds me I'll need to go back
to the market next week for trailing lobelia. A flowerbox isn't a
flowerbox without trailing lobelia up front.

Forty-four flats will take care of the front yard. I'll need another
60 flats for the back. But not all marigolds and lobelia. I'll want
some miniature dahlias for the back — pink and yellow. That's just
how Ned liked it. Ned was particular when it came to the garden. "I
can't take too much yellow," he used to say. "All that glare hurts my
eyes."

I like the flowers lined up just so. I like them spaced out evenly,
with about three inches between each plant. Three inches gives them
enough room to spread out, but it also means the flowerbeds look
nice and full. If there's one thing I can't bear to look at it's a
flowerbed with big empty spots. Or one that's all jumbled together.

Terry next door (Why is it all the young women these days have
names a man could have, too?) doesn't bother lining up her flowers.
"I enjoy chaos," she told me the other day when she was getting out

of her car. "Don't get me wrong, Isabelle, your garden's lovely. It's just a little more orderly than a person like me could ever manage."

I suppose by a person like herself, she meant a doctor and a mum. She's an accomplished woman, all right, an anesthesiologist, but I'd like her better if her garden looked a little, well, tidier, I guess.

I've always enjoyed tending the garden. It was something Ned and I liked to do together. Of course, I did most of the tending. Ned would sit on the porch, nursing his beer, but he'd let me know when something didn't look quite right. "You've got too much space between those marigolds!" he'd holler. "What on earth's wrong with you, Isabelle?"

I like working in the garden, letting my fingers scoop up the dark soil. I like the tender green colour of the new plants and the way they get greener and hardier looking as the summer goes along. But mostly I like how the garden looks when it's all planted and everything's in its right place. Which reminds me I've got to bring the plastic fawn up from the basement and put it under the elm tree, off to the left a little. That's how Ned liked it. He used to say how looking out the kitchen window and seeing that fawn first thing in the morning made him feel like he lived in the country. It makes me glad to think of Ned enjoying himself like that.

The end wasn't pretty.

I try not to think about it. Ned lying in that narrow bed on the fifth floor at the Jewish General Hospital, hooked up to an IV drip, him looking as thin as our elm tree in the dead of winter.

It's better for me to think about the garden and the chores that still have to get done. It was always better for me to concentrate on my chores than to think about things. Harder things. Not that chores aren't hard, especially for a woman my age. I still do all the cleaning. I try to do the heavy work in winter. That's when I wax the floors — upstairs and downstairs both — straighten out the closets, and polish Ned's mum's silver, every inch of it till it gleams.

I wait for spring to air the pillows and wash the curtains and bedspreads. That way I can hang things out. Nothing smells as good to me as laundry that's just come in from the line. Ned used to laugh at me when he came to bed at night and I'd try to get him to sniff the sheets. "Just smell them, Ned," I'd say and he'd start laughing. "They smell like sheets, Isabelle — sheets for goodness sake."

It used to bother me when Ned talked like that — when he didn't make an effort to see things my way. But now that he's gone and there's a big empty spot in the bed next to me, I even miss how Ned used to laugh at me.

He wasn't a bad man, Ned wasn't. And he was handsome in his day, too. Handsomer than any man I'd ever seen, though then again, I hadn't seen too many. I was just a slip of a girl when I met him. And a farm girl, too. What did I know coming from my mum and dad's place in the Gaspé? The only boys I'd ever seen were the ones at school and from the other farms near ours. A couple of those boys weren't even all right in the head. Like that Leonard Blanquette, who used to get the shakes when the teacher asked him a question. How my cousin Nan and I laughed about Leonard. Really, it wasn't too kind of us.

Nowadays, they'd put a boy like Leonard in a remedial class or say he had ADD. Seems half the kids today have ADD. Terry was telling me her little boy's got it and he's getting special treatment for it. Must be costing her and her husband a fortune, but with both of them being doctors, I figure they can afford it.

My cousin Nan was the one who brought me to the legion party where I met Ned. She'd been to Montreal before, but it was my first time. I nearly lost my balance when Nan and I walked along Ste. Catherine Street. I'd never seen so many lights and buildings, and so many people all at once, all of them looking like they were heading off to someplace important.

Ned used to say he picked me out the second Nan and I walked into that legion hall. "There was something about you, Isabelle. Something sweet and innocent. And your legs... your legs weren't too bad, either. Long legs like a colt's." I used to like when Ned talked like that. It'd bring me back to the first night we met, and then to the way he'd courted me. Brought me flowers and introduced me to his mum. Told her I was the girl he was going to marry. Looking back on it, I figure I didn't have much choice in the matter.

Terry next door she never met Ned. She and her husband and their brood — they've got three kids — two girls and the boy with ADD… imagine having three kids and holding down a job, too — they moved in the summer after Ned passed on. In a way, it's just as well he didn't know them. He wouldn't have liked the way Terry and her husband let those kids run wild. Knowing Ned, he'd have insisted on putting up a fence — a high one, too — between our house and theirs. And the noise those kids make, well that kind of noise would have driven Ned right over the edge. Ned was particular about noise. Lucky for us Mikey was a quiet child. Never minded playing by himself in his room. I can't imagine any of Terry's kids playing by themselves that way.

Ned wasn't just particular about marigolds and noise. He was particular about most things. Wanted them done his way. I suppose it was his mum's fault. She spoiled him something awful, especially after his dad died. It used to bother me when she went on about Ned the way she used to — as if she thought he was the Christ child made flesh.

Still, I don't like people speaking ill of Ned. I get the feeling Terry doesn't think too highly of him — which isn't fair considering the two of them never even met. I think maybe she heard something from the other neighbours. You know how people get to talking. Maybe someone said something about how Ned sometimes drank too much. So I made a point of showing Terry the cards — birthday cards, Valentine's Day cards and Mother's Day cards. Forty-nine years' worth. Ned never missed a special occasion and I kept all his cards, each and every one.

Those cards still make me tear up when I look at them. "A wife is a friend for life." "To my sweetheart on her special day." "You make my life complete." Sometimes I wonder about the folks at Hallmark who write those cards and what their lives must be like. Imagine being able to come up with flowery words like that! It's poetry is what it is.

"Do you mind if I look at what he wrote inside?" Terry asked when I brought the box of cards over to her house.

Her question caught me by surprise. "He didn't write anything," I told her. "He just signed his name. Look, you can see for yourself," I said, opening the Mother's Day card from the year he died (I keep the cards in the exact order he gave them to me and each one's still in its envelope), "it says, 'Ned.'"

A wave of longing passed through me when I looked at Ned's spidery handwriting.

Terry looked kind of sheepish when I showed her the inside of the card. It made me wonder if maybe that husband of hers doesn't remember special occasions the way Ned did.

"I guess you must get pretty lonely, Isabelle," Terry said then. We were sitting on the couch in her living room. Terry's got one of those modern couches (down-filled she told me, as if she thought filling a couch with down was a brilliant idea, when the truth is, a person — especially one my age — practically needs a crane to pick himself up from that couch of hers.)

"I don't have time to be lonely," I told her. "I've got too many chores to do — and the garden to tend. In my younger days, I made preserves, too. Pickles and relish and crab apple jelly in the fall. I used to line up the jars on the shelves in our cold room downstairs. Made me feel like I was ready to face the winter months ahead. I've always liked being organized."

As soon as the words were out of my mouth, I regretted saying them. Anyone could see from Terry's house that being organized wasn't exactly her strong suit. There was a laundry basket full of kids' clothes smack in the middle of the front hallway and though I'd spotted a toy trunk in the corner of the living room, there were toys all over the place — a doll with shiny pink lips next to me on the couch, a plastic lawnmower in front of the fireplace, and jigsaw puzzle pieces on the living room carpet.

"Lorraine down the street told me you and Ned were married nearly 50 years," Terry went on.

"That's right," I said, "nearly 50 years. It's a lifetime, really." The whole time I was thinking to myself how Lorraine must've been the one to say something nasty about Ned. She was just the type to speak ill of the dead.

"I can't imagine being married for 50 years," Terry said. "How did you manage?" She looked up at me then and I got the feeling she really wanted to know.

How did I manage?

"It took a lot of give and take," I told her. Yes, that was a fair answer. I'd certainly done a lot of giving with Ned; the taking, well, the taking, I hadn't been so good at. But I didn't need to tell Terry that. Especially not if Lorraine had been gossiping about Ned.

The doorbell rang. It was Terry's kids, all three of them home at once. She rushed to answer the door, all smiles, and I tried to pull myself up off that down-filled couch of hers. But I kept sinking back into it. I didn't want to have to ask for help and I didn't want to wear out my welcome, either. So I tried again.

This time, I planted my hands down next to me and tried hoisting myself up. I'd have made it if it hadn't been for Ned's cards. I remembered them at the last second and when I tried to reach out for them, the doll with the shiny pink lips tumbled to the floor and I tripped over her.

It was the little boy — the one with ADD — who came running over first. Not that I remember, but Terry told me afterwards. I hit my forehead on the coffee table and that must've put me out cold. It was the little boy who went to the freezer for ice. It's a good thing Terry's a doctor, because she knew what to do. She used a cloth to stop the bleeding; the ice was for the swelling afterwards. And I do remember her looking into my eyes and asking me if I could see her hand when she waved it in front of my face.

The worst part wasn't the gash on my forehead — or even that I wet my pants when I was lying on the floor, though that was pretty bad. No, the worst part was talking to the little boy afterwards.

He and the sisters were carrying on in the backyard and I was thinking how maybe a fence wasn't the worst idea in the world. They were playing Hide 'n Seek and he came running over to our garden — I should say "my garden," but I still can't get used to it, not even after all this time.

He was out of breath when he came over. "Isabelle," he said, pointing to the flowerpot on the porch where I was sitting, "can I hide over there?"

I thought about telling him I didn't think it was right for a child to call me Isabelle, and how in my day, we called adults Mr. and Mrs. such and such. But then I remembered how he'd been the one to fetch the ice from the freezer and I changed my mind. "Sure," I told him, moving my green plastic garden chair over a little so he could get by, "go hide behind the flowerpot. Besides that way, you can keep me company."

I could hear the big sister counting in their yard. "...Four, three, two, one. Hide 'n seek! Here I come!"

I felt a prickle of excitement shoot down my spine. I hoped she wouldn't find the little boy. At least not right away. I opened up the newspaper I'd brought outside with me and started reading a recipe for asparagus soup. It's full of vitamins, asparagus is.

"You must get lonesome, Isabelle." At first, the little voice coming from behind the flowerpot took me by surprise. A small sad voice. "Mom says your boy lives far away and he only comes to visit at Christmas."

My boy, my Mikey. Had he ever been as small as this tyke from next door? If only I could remember those days better, bring them back.

"I do get lonesome. Oh so lonesome." The words fell out of me.

"You called me Ned that day you tripped over the doll," the voice continued.

"I did?" My cheeks burned behind the newspaper.

"He was your husband, right?"

"Yes, he was. For nearly 50 years. We were about to celebrate our golden anniversary when he died. He was so sick." I could hear my voice crack. What was wrong with me talking to a little boy like this?

I cleared my throat. Loudly, so he'd get the message to hush up.

At first, he was quiet, but then he started up again. "It felt weird when you called me Ned. And you know, you pushed me, too."

I turned to the flowerpot. "I didn't push you."

"Oh, yes, you did. Hard. Real hard. You told me to leave you alone. You told me never to lay a hand on you again. Mum says it's 'cuz Ned used to smack you."

I gulped for air.

"He shouldn't have done that, Isabelle."

"I found you! I found you!" the big sister hollered. The other sister had been hiding in their shed. Now the two of them were headed over in my direction. The big one put her hands on her hips. "Have you seen my brother?" she asked.

"No fair!" the voice whispered from behind the flowerpot.

I pretended to fuss with the newspaper, folding it along the creases so it'd lie flat the way I liked it. "Nope," I told the girls. "Haven't seen him all day." Then I got up from my green garden chair. My legs wobbled a little, but that didn't stop me.

I looked out at the garden — the rows of dahlias and lobelia and marigolds, the fawn under the elm tree. The fawn wasn't quite in his spot.

I could go down into the garden and scoot him over a touch.

Or maybe I wouldn't bother. Maybe I'd let him stay just where he was.

Missing Pieces

Sheryl Halpern

Missing Pieces

I chose the worst possible day and time to go back to the mall. A mid-December Saturday, around one o'clock. But the contract work had piled up, Paul wouldn't let me drive our new car, and we were leaving in a few days for a delightful holiday gathering with hot-and-cold running in-laws and assorted cousins. So that meant bringing Paul along, who was always so enthusiastic about shopping (unless he could check out computers) and our five-year-old, Anita. It meant getting out of comfort clothes and into presentable stuff, putting on heavy coats and snow boots and hats. It also meant making a wide detour around the week-old Santa Claus Train display in the centre of the mall. Bad timing, all around.

But I had my list of things that had to be done by someone (translation: me), and I was already starting to tick off errands. I had to return an electronic kitchen scale — an anniversary gift, so I could weigh my food electronically — to Priceway before the 30-day no-sweat-returns period was up and it had to be mailed to the manufacturer. The Diet Magic scale had developed problems: when you picked it up, it made a *chik chik* noise inside, like dried peas rattling, that said it was broken or missing pieces (or else I really did have five-pound apples.) Then I had to get a new plant water-meter to replace the old one (when the watering was Paul's job, the plant-watchers had that straight-from-NASA look; I'd get a cheap one.) Then get Anita's new jeans, and a gift for her friend Tania. Then get to the ATM, get cash, pay the phone bill and charge cards.

We got inside and I unzipped Anita's quilted purple overcoat and threw it over one arm. It weighed about what the kitchen scale weighed; I was balanced. "Can you take Anita with you to the computer store? We could meet back here in half an hour, no make that forty-five minutes."

"Why do you need forty-five minutes to return something?" asked Paul.

"You haven't seen the lines. Just getting there will be fun. I'll meet you near the T-shirt place. Anita, you stay with Daddy this time."

"Then I'll go on the Santa Claus Train and get ice cream?" Anita asked.

I'm really not good at bribes. "Well, no promises. We'll see if things are still crowded then, Nita."

"I'm not taking her, Terry. I need a break. I need some time to myself. This is my one day off; you get all week to relax," said Paul.

"You think I spend all week relaxing? You think that the floors got washed and the beds made and the research work for Allied Industries faxed in and dinner made and Nita and her friends carpooled — all while I was relaxing? You think I eat bonbons all day?" I had spots in front of my eyes, I was so mad. "And look at this list! Do you have a list of things to do? What do you have to do at the mall?"

"You always have lists," said Paul. "And you only have a part-time job. I work all day, every day. Look, you wanted to come here, and I need an hour. I'll take her at two or so, meet me at the TV store."

"One hour, right?" I said, magnanimous in defeat. "You'll be there and watch her?"

"I'm going with Mommy," Nita sang as we swung off. I stopped and threw her pompom hat into my shopping bag. Now off to Priceway, where the prices make your day.

If only the scale had worked. Paul had said, "Why don't you let me fix it?" but I knew the drill. First, one Saturday in his workshop cubbyhole so he could take it apart and become frustrated. Then three weeks in bite-sized pieces on the shelf, and if I tentatively asked when it would be ready I'd get my head back in slices. Along with a lecture about nagging him over trivia. Whatever. So. Fix the scale problem. Return it today, buy the new one later. Fix the weight problem after the holidays (ten pounds off — okay, five — would be good, getting close to pre-Anita weight.) Fix life. Get one to-do list closer to a happy ending. Right.

Getting to Customer Service with Anita was like taking a piece of living Velcro through the store. Things stuck to her — a chocolate bar, a Princess Zora action figure, an impractical lacy nightgown, size 12. We'd stop, I'd explain in calm caregiver tones why we didn't need it and to put it back, and then I'd promise a treat later. In my coat pocket was one of those prizes you get out of a gumball machine. I felt I might have to use it.

There were four people ahead of me in line, and we had to get a number. After I tore one off, Anita pulled six out and danced around, bowing and saying, "For you, ladies and gentlemen," and passing them out. The woman in front of me, bless her, had three different items to return, each requiring its own hand-written return slip. But finally, after waiting, showing a bill, my Priceway card and, I guess, my temper, I got a credit for the scale. "Don't we get anything here, Mommy?" said Anita, as we started to leave. "No, we get to give things back," I said.

Grabbed Nita and without totally dislocating her shoulder, ran down the plant aisle with her and got the waterer on special. Unfortunately we did have to pass a candy display on the way to the cash and I told her that if she stamped like that again, she could forget about the ice cream. "Ever?" she said, lip trembling. "No," I said, "just today. But if you act nicely, you still can have it today."

In line she was, of course, an angel, saying hello to a little boy in a Snuggly and an old lady with a walker, and as I was paying, the grandmotherly cashier said, "You know, dear, she's too friendly. You shouldn't let her talk to everyone like that. She should be afraid of strangers." "I don't usually," I began, "but she's with me right now." "Well, I admit my own were like that, but she'll have to learn," said the cashier. "Of course," I said, momentarily wishing I could leave Nita with the grandma at the register, a total stranger, for five minutes, just five. But we had to run into the discount store next door to pick up the size 6X jeans to replace the pair with patches on the patches. Anita liked them, which was something, but she also wanted to stay and talk to a boy in the socks section because "he's my new friend and we want to play together."

When we got to the ATM I let her take one of the bank envelopes, and she let me pay the bills, fair trade. By now the hour was almost up, and as we walked out into the mall I took a deep drag of the incense and chocolate and let the golden lights of the brass store and the gift boutiques fill me. "Mommy, can I tell you something?" "What, Anita?" I said, feeling motherly. "Do you want to hear a really gross joke? Jamie told me, it's from TV." "No, not really, dear," executing a quick about-face at the first faint ho-ho-ho up ahead. No Santa today. Been there, done that, got the Elf Photo. "You never want to hear anything," she pouted.

We got to the TV store about one minute before Paul arrived, and the prisoner changed hands ("Now I can have my ice cream, right Daddy? You promised.") Paul's firmer; he looked down and told Nita, "I said we might get an ice cream, but first we're going to look at computer games, okay?" Then he said to me, "How long?" I calculated, ten minutes to my favourite boutique, ten back, twenty to shop, and five minutes leeway, and said "Forty-five minutes." "Okay," said Paul. "Fair enough, but I'm not taking her coat, I'll lose it somewhere, and you have no distractions. Meet you at Tee Tops."

I watched as Paul dragged her off, protesting — there goes the prisoner — then I trudged off with her coat and my mantra — I must not lose this coat I must not lose this coat. Anita had already lost one sweatshirt at kindergarten. How can you lose an oversized hot pink top with "Princess ZORA" and little gold crowns printed on it? Trust me, it can be done. But the coat, a hand-me-down from a cousin, had to last the winter. I took off my jacket and knotted the sleeves around it.

The next half-hour went a bit quicker, and as I left the boutique, virtuous for having resisted everything, I checked my watch. I had fifteen minutes left. Good. I headed to Tee Tops.

I like spotting Paul from far away; it's like seeing a familiar landmark, getting near home. I saw him from halfway down the ramp, huddled up on a bench, still zipped up to his beard in his bulky tan down jacket. Balding and thin-faced, he didn't quite look like a GQ ad. But he was mine. I walked faster, trying not to whack anyone with my bags. I felt a second of guilt, he was getting a cold, and I'd dragged him out, he should be back in bed — and then realized he was reading one of the sci-fi novels he brought to the mall in self-defense and had forgotten where he was. Anita wasn't jumping up and down on him — at least that. Probably talking to the T-shirt man. "Hi, there, handsome, can I buy you a hot chocolate?" I said, plumping down beside him on the bench, coats, bags and all. "I see we're alone at last. Where's Nita?" He looked up from his book, and said in an almost ordinary voice, "I don't know."

I looked at him; he was holding onto the book, trying to read another page. There was a blankness to him. And the only child nearby was someone else's little boy in a stroller.

"You don't know where Anita is?"

"I'm not sure — I thought she might have run off to see you," he said. "She's not around here. I looked."

Sometimes I don't hear things, because my mind is somewhere else, and I'm not concentrating. I wasn't sure that he'd said "she's not here," so I asked him to repeat himself. He did, looking down at the terrazzo. I didn't believe him. But she wasn't there. It was like stopping a videotape on just one frame. I could see her as if she were there, pulling my arm somewhere. Her curly hair, which she wouldn't let me brush this morning, and her matching deer-brown eyes, and the light flecks of freckles over her nose. I'd let her wear her pink outfit with the flocked hearts which was getting too short on her, I'd have to —. Her puffy white snow boots. I could see the half-fierce scowl that she shot me when I told her to get ready and turn the TV off. I could see her and even feel her in front of me. I found myself holding her coat to me, the way mothers on the news did when they picked up lost toddlers. Like them, I'd probably scream at her and cry. Was I overreacting? She would not be allowed to stay up late tonight, that's for certain.

I looked around. Overhead there were gold star cutouts and floss-headed angels dancing in the mall air currents, and Peace on Earth banners with fancy script in green and white. I kept thinking I could see her coming down the ramp, out of the corner of my eye, and kept jerking around to catch her. Maybe the coat was all that was left, all I was going to have, and my lists of what she needed. But the birthday party Sunday at two, but Dr. Ryan on Monday. All the appointments started fading off the calendar. I felt hot and cold and things slowed down to dreamlike. I would be calling detectives, psychics. They would console me, get the details, shake their heads.

"What do you mean, you've looked? Wasn't she with you? Where did you leave her? Where is she?" I wanted to run after her, but my legs wouldn't work.

"She was cranky, she wanted a snack, and I didn't have anything for her, you didn't pack anything. When we passed the arcade, she started pestering me about playing the games. I gave her four quarters. I left her there just for a minute while I went into the electronics shop, I told her not to leave, but when I came back, she was gone. She'd wandered off."

"But where were you?" I asked, as if that mattered. "I was checking out the new *Island of Doom* version, and uh, the *Schoolbus Stories* CDs too," he added. "And that copier you keep talking about, you can probably deduct it as an expense."

"But Anita —"

"I'm sure she'll come back, she knows where I am," he said. "One of us has to stay here, or she'll panic, she'll be really lost."

I could feel the weight of Anita's coat on my arm, the shopping bag with her new pants (and I forgot to shop for the birthday party gift, and markers for school) and I thought, no, nothing can change, it can't all go away, I've got her coat.

"Besides, how far could she have gone in five minutes? She'll get worried, she'll cry, but it will be a good lesson for her. She'll learn an important lesson," Paul said.

Yes, very educational. Let's leave her alone in the mall, let's let her walk into traffic. Services for the child who learned her lesson will be held at 2 p.m. If I'd still had the scale in its bag I would have swung it at him. I think. I stood up and dropped all my bags on the bench.

"When did you miss her?" I asked, sounding drained-dry, flat. Get the facts. No. Stop talking. Wake up.

"Well, about half an hour — but I've been looking for her. It's a small shopping centre. I checked all the stores near here, went in and out and down the aisles of the hardware place, the grocery, that earring boutique, no one's seen her but they'll keep an eye out. I just sat down a minute ago, needed a break."

"Let's call the police!" The phones were ten stores up, there was time. I'd be calm, I'd explain and I had a picture from her kindergarten in my wallet, and one for her library card. If we did it quickly, they said the first hours were critical.

"You're a worrier, Terry. You always jump to the worst conclusions. I've spoken to the security guards, gave Anita's description, they'll be looking for her, she was wearing her purple playsuit, wasn't she? Oh, I — wait a second."

"Wait what?"

"She kept after me for ice cream, I didn't think about that till now —"

"You stay there, then," I said, patting him on the shoulder and heading off. He was paralyzed, he was stunned, I couldn't move him.

I kept wanting to rewind the afternoon, take a taxi and leave Anita and Paul at home with videos, or not leave Anita with Paul in the computer shop. I shouldn't have, I shouldn't have, he couldn't watch her for half an hour, he wasn't fit to watch goldfish, he just looked like a father in family pictures. I ran to the food court, but it felt like wading through marshland. As though I weren't really moving through the swaddled crowds, the bright red and green stores, the warm incense smells, the brassy carols. I got there, I got there, and took two seconds to clear away the bright lights and get my breath back, and then I didn't want to look, because I wouldn't find her. She wouldn't be there because I wanted her to be there. That's what happens.

But like a daydream, there she was, near Muffin Man, sitting at a white metal patio table by herself, dangling her legs. I ran over, before she could disappear. I put my arms around her to be sure. She gave me her favourite new glower (eyebrows drawn low, lips tight) and fought her way out.

"He was getting me ice cream, and now he won't," she complained.

"Now he won't?"

"He won't! I was waiting and waiting for you. You said we could have ice cream. The big kids wouldn't let me play the whirlybird game, so I came here and I was sitting and sitting and no one came and then a man said don't cry, I'll get you ice cream."

"Where is he? Where's the man who was getting you ice cream, Anita?" I sounded too alarmed, too parent-like. Lassie come home.

"It's too late, he's not here anymore," she yelled, turning red and bursting into tears. "It's all your fault! He said I could have a chocolate chocolate cone, and now you're here, so I won't get it!"

"Anita, he was a stranger, he could have hurt you. Remember we told you about strangers?"

"But he was nice, and he said he probably knew you and Daddy, so he wasn't a stranger, he was a friend."

Grabbing her by the hand, I pulled her up and did a circuit of the food court, but Anita didn't see her man anywhere. After I got her back in her coat (I left it unzipped, but I had to put it back on her, it was breaking my arm), I got her a chocolate chocolate cone — I know, I know, I shouldn't have, mixed messages, but to stop her crying, to keep her from looking for nice strangers. I got myself one too, and gave the abridged version of the police station's *Never Talk to Strangers* booklet while we hurried back to Paul. On the way back I began seeing things his way, making excuses. Things had turned out all right, he was tired and distracted, she'd just run away, it was her fault. But still.

He was on the bench near the T-shirts, and he jumped up, going from pale and still to his standard self in sixty seconds.

"You found her!" he said. "You found her! See, nothing happened. Where was she?"

"Near Muffin Man, waiting for an ice cream from a man she met. Paul —"

"A man? Did you see him? He probably saw you and skipped out. Were we lucky, he could have been long gone. Good thing you got there in time. Nothing happened."

"Something did! Something happened!" I shouted.

He pushed me onto the bench. "Nothing happened, Terry, nothing. She's okay. We don't have to call 911. We don't have to put up posters. We're lucky. She learned a good lesson. Come on, calm down, don't get hysterical. It's all right. Let's sit here for a minute. Anita, you learned your lesson, right? Don't talk to strangers. I see you got your ice cream." He sounded murmury, soothing. He could always calm me that way.

I looked at him and, through all the muzak and the buzzing in my ears, I heard a rattly noise. *Chik chik.* I heard it clearly.

Taxi

Jill Goldberg

Taxi

You never know who you'll meet when you drive a taxi. I should know, I was born in one.

My father is a taxi driver, has been for nearly 25 years, and I've been driving one for two and half. It's not a family tradition exactly, but you could say that I've got an instinct for city navigation the way migratory birds know when to fly South; it's in my nature.

My father's name is Luca, mine is Christmas, and I have no idea what my mother's name is. I never knew her, barely even met her. My father, who isn't my real father has been mother and father to me, and his cheerful presence has never left room for regret or lamentation about what I was missing.

My father loves his taxi. He takes pride in it like an old-fashioned housewife loves her home. He keeps it clean and neat outside and in. He vacuums it daily, polishes the steering wheel, always has a fresh box of tissues and it never, ever smells stale. His cab gleams like a sunny day.

I was born on the night of a blizzard. If you know Montreal, you'll know that when it snows, it can snow steadily and heavily for hours. And so it did on December 25, 1973 making for a really white Christmas during which most people stayed safely, cozily in their homes.

It wasn't late at night, only 6:30, but it was so dark and the roads so forbidding that it seemed much later. Although my father didn't have to work, he was still driving around looking for customers, keeping himself cheerful by singing loudly along with the scratchy tape of Russian folk music he liked to play in his cab. Sometimes he got so involved with the music he'd bang his steering wheel with pleasure. He didn't like to think of people stranded in a blizzard, and since he was pretty new to Canada, and had no family of his own, he figured he might as well keep driving around, looking for customers who might need his service. I think he fancied himself a kind of hero with four wheels. As he was driving north on Park Avenue, a woman hailed him and he pulled over. The roads were slippery with fresh snow and the visibility was poor, so my father took his time pulling up to the curb, while the woman, who is my mother, waved frantically at him.

Although the Royal Victoria Hospital was closer, and the roads were terrible and the driving slow, my mother insisted on going to The Jewish General. She held her belly, which was well hidden under layers of heavy clothes, and moaned, but otherwise she said little. The drive, which should have taken just 10 minutes, took 45 minutes of careful maneuvering, and by the time my father pulled up in front of the emergency room, I was already showing my head. My father took one look at what was going on in his taxi and unlike many men who would have panicked, my jubilant father called out, "Congratulations!" And with that, I came into the world. As my father tells it, he felt the joy of a new father as he scurried into the emergency ward and called for help. I can imagine the giddy, excited and happy look on his face; my father is a very jovial man, and he must have felt that my arrival was, in some way, an auspicious omen or a tribute to the beloved taxi he kept up so well.

With my father prancing by her side, my mother and I were taken into the hospital, where I was washed and checked for the usual signs of health and anything unusual that could befall an infant born in a taxi. Once a nurse determined that I was fine, I was swaddled up, and at that moment my father was so moved by my mother's angelic face that he fell on his knees and declared his love for her. My mother responded by looking at him sweetly, angelically, and saying "Merry Christmas." For some reason he mistook my mother's words to be the name she wanted to give to me. Because of this brief exchange, on my birth certificate, written up a few days later, my name is proudly written as "Merry Christmas". Given the choices, I decided I'd go by Christmas. A strange name, I know, but it seemed like one of the few ways I had of marking my unusual birth that happened on that Christmas day.

While my effusive father went to the hospital cafeteria to get a celebratory Coca-Cola and doughnut for my mother, she filled out all the preliminary paperwork to do with my birth. She must have seen my father's name on his identity card in his taxi because, in spite of the ordeal of having just given birth in a taxi during a blizzard, she had the wherewithal, unbeknownst to anyone but herself, to register one proud Luca Lyubov as my legal guardian and father.

The next day, my father showed up at the hospital to visit my mother, but when he went to the maternity ward, the nurses there told him that she'd disappeared in the night. Left without any clue about who she was or where she was going. They told him that she must have snuck down the stairs and out any one of the hospital's doors. They didn't know much more about her than he did, but they knew she was gone. My father used his poor English as an excuse to avoid the probing questions and pointed looks that followed, saying only "Don't worry, she'll come home."

With that, they gave my stunned, but undeterred father a sympathetic look and went to get me from the nursery. As they put the bundle that was me in his arms, they tried to give him some lessons in infant care. This was before the days when an infant couldn't leave the hospital without a car seat, and so my father was sent off with a bag full of formula, a few diapers and very little else besides his eager spirit.

My father is not one to get upset easily, and I'm sure he would have taken this development in stride; still, I chuckle when I think of him placing me in the back seat of the car and attempting to belt me in. He says that I barely whimpered, and, in fact, was calm, even curious the whole way home. He talked to me all the way, describing his senile mother, his homeland; telling me, cheerfully, what a happy life we were going to lead. It apparently didn't occur to him once that he was in a troubling situation, or that he should look for my mother in any conventional way. My father is from Russia, a place where he learned not to trust the authorities, and so he, a single man without any knowledge of babies, had decided to bring me up himself and, indeed, he felt absolutely sure that he'd find my mother himself, too. He really believed that he'd rescue her, and we'd all be reunited romantically, happily ever after. He knew it was just a matter of time. In the meantime, he wanted to introduce me to his friends and acquaintances: a raucous group of immigrant men that he knew from the local café.

So, Luca went off to the neighborhood café and brought me along, dutifully wrapping me up first. He put his own socks on my feet and arms, an enormous hat covered my head, and the rest of me was covered and wrapped in blankets tied with scarves. Finally, I was put in a pillowcase and brought to his friends. There is only one yellowing picture of me from this day, and I look as round and as padded as a baby seal.

I was presented at the café, amidst much uproar, and once they all got over their shock, the cafe owner passed out several rounds of drinks. My introduction to the world of immigrant men was one of slightly drunken revelry, festiveness and warmth. My father tells me that a baby born in the new country is considered a sign of prosperity, and the men congratulated my father with slaps on the back and cigars as if he really were my father. Happily, the more practical and more experienced wives of my father's friends and acquaintances stepped in and collected what they thought we'd need: clothes, bottles, a used high chair. Someone even gave me a lovely yellow knit blanket with a rabbit and a duck on it that I still have, but the most crucial donation was perhaps the used car seat that served as my ticket to this funny life I've led, in and out of cabs.

I can't tell you much about my babyhood because of course I don't remember it. But, I do know two things: my father kept driving his taxi, and he took me everywhere. He told all his passengers that I was his best customer, and that I always tipped well. And so, strapped into my car seat, and later in the passenger seat of the taxi, I saw the city through the window of a cab for the first six years of my life. By time I was four I could navigate most major streets of Montreal, and by time I started school, I could chat to customers in both English and French and use the taxi radio. Sometimes when a call was put out for a taxi at a particular address, I'd be the one to respond. I guess I became kind of like the taxi company pet — the dispatcher would come over the radio and say "Passenger for Christmas", and he'd give me an address. I'd answer back, and on we drove, laughter keeping our wheels turning. When I think back on it, I'm sure that my child's voice over the radio was a source of much amusement for all the cab drivers who could hear our antics.

You should know that my father had a whole life before he was a taxi driver. His profession in Russia was a circus lion tamer. His wasn't a well-known circus, and jobs for lion tamers were scarce. So, when the circus went under, my father lied about his profession, and made his way to Canada. To this day, he loves the circus and he loves circus animals. In fact, the last lion he tamed now lives with us in the form of a head mounted on the wall, and his hide covering our living room floor. My father still talks to the lion and often he gets up from the dinner table and says to me, "Now I will show you how to treat a lion!" Then he laughs so hard that he shakes uncontrollably as he sticks his head in the lion's permanently open jaws and calls out, "You see, you see, Christmas! You have to CHARM the lion. I am a lion CHARMER.! This lion is the most ferocious of all!" He laughs uproariously at his joke. He always finishes his routine by telling me that my mother, when she comes back to us, will love this lion like he does, she will love the three of us as her own family. He has other rituals too. His favorite pastime is to watch grainy old videos of his circus. Every Sunday night he fries two sausages, drinks a cup of instant coffee and puts in one from a selection of very old videos. We sit together on the couch and watch as my father and his former colleagues, wearing outlandish, cheap-looking costumes, entertain masses of children and their parents. My father had a special respect for the elephant trainer. The circus always opened with the dancing elephants who would trot around the ring and stop in time to the music, dancing on their back legs. Every Sunday night it's the same thing, elephants dancing to Tchaikovsky, and my father laughing with abandon until he weeps and cries out, "Look, Christmas, look, do you see the elephants? Look at them dance!" And he laughs so hard it must hurt, and then he ends the evening with a sigh: "Those were good days." Soon after that he usually falls asleep on the couch snoring loudly, and presumably dreaming of dancing elephants and roaring lions.

It's hard for me to imagine that they were very good days. My young father sticking his head in a lion's mouth night after night, all the while being paid in little more than cigarettes. Yet, it seems like he was in love with the life, with the companionship of the circus.

*

Given everything I've told you about my childhood, I suppose it should come as no surprise that when I finished high school at 18, I became a taxi driver. At first I thought it was just to make enough money to go to college. But now I am 21 and I'm still driving my cab. I like the calm and the freedom. I like the eccentric examples of humanity that come in and out of my cab, all the thousands of possible interactions, and mostly I like zipping up the city streets, the challenge of finding the fastest way to a given point on the map. These streets feel like they're mine, supple, bending to my knowledge of them.

My father has always told me that when I was old enough, we'd look for my mother. Unlike some people who might dread this, my father welcomes the opportunity to bring someone else into our little family. He tenderly nurtures this peculiar fantasy that one day we'll welcome a stranger into our lives as my mother. He even jokes that I am beautiful, just like my mother, and he says that she'll be so proud to see me, so proud of all I've become. My father's devotion to me is blind, and his certainty that one day we'll be a happy family of three is absolute.

On my 21st birthday, he brings me a cake and, to make things festive, we watch back to back videos of him thrusting his head into the lion's mouth. All the while, my father grins and cackles and sometimes talks to the real lion mounted on the wall. "You bad boy, too lazy to chew my head, Mr. Lion!"

Just before I go to bed that night, my father announces that he has done something else for my birthday. What he has done is made signs with my baby picture on them saying "If your baby was born on December 25th, 1973, call…" He has left his phone number on the sign and at the bottom of the sign he has written "Free Ride!" His eyes shine as he tells me that because he drives a taxi, he'll be able to pick my mother up, anywhere, anytime, no charge. She will ride, like a queen, straight to her long lost family

The very next day, in spite of the winter chill, my father plasters signs at bus stations, metro stations, on telephone poles, up and down Park Avenue where my mother first hailed my willing father down, and brought the two of us, me and Luca together.

I'm sure the signs must seem odd, and probably even a little sad to most who see them. But this isn't the point, and his ingenious idea brings my father far too much pleasure to let this matter.

At first no one calls, but we're neither surprised nor deterred. As New Year's draws near, the weather takes a turn and becomes brutally cold, as it does in Montreal at this time of year. And it is on one of the coldest days of the year that the phone rings.

"Come get me," croaks a strange sounding voice. "I need a ride."

When, after 21 years of waiting for a reunion, we finally pick her up in my father's very ready taxi, it is immediately clear that the woman who called is definitely not my mother. I know this right away because she's black and at least 70 or more and has obviously called the number on the sign out of delirium or desperation, but not because she was looking for a family reunion. But it is quite clear that this woman needs us, and I wonder if she used her last quarter to call. She looks like she might not have slept indoors in some time, her eyes a bit unfocused, her speech a bit slurred. Her clothes are ragged, some teeth are missing, and she has a bruise over her left cheekbone that, even on her dark skin, looks like it hurts.

So, 21 years after I was born there, my father and I take this strange woman to the hospital. All together, the three of us go into the emergency ward and wait. Since she's not considered to be in danger, the wait is long before she gets any attention, and when she finally does, and the doctor asks what our relationship is to this woman, I say, without hesitation, "She's my mother." If the doctor doesn't believe me, he says nothing, and lets me know that she will be okay. They've cleaned her up, given her something to eat, and she'll stay there for the night.

We go home and if I feel sad for what has happened on that day, my father feels the full weight of so many years of hope collapsing inside him. He so badly wanted to give me my mother for my birthday. But more than that, he simply hadn't equipped himself for the possibility or certain reality that his dream of reunion would be disappointed.

The next morning we return to the hospital and ask to see the woman we'd dropped off the day before. It isn't a surprise, but still it lands heavily, when the nurse tells us she's gone. Without a trace. That she just walked out the door without telling anyone, and they don't know where she went to or how she set out.

Although it's a Tuesday, my father spends the afternoon watching his elephant and lion videos. This time he's not laughing, he's mumbling to himself in Russian, holding his heavy head in his hands. After he has watched all his videos, he takes the lion's head off the wall and curls up on the couch with his own head deep inside its jaws and falls into a heavy, gently snoring sleep.

Quietly, I sit down beside him on the couch and watch over him, all the while feeling mournful for a loss of a hope I never knew I had. Then, I cover him with a blanket, turn out the light, and leave him to sleep while I go out to take down the remaining signs, printed on bright orange paper, most of them too tattered by the harsh weather to be read by now, and none of them likely to make our little family of two grow any larger.

La Maison Américaine

Philip Dann

La Maison Américaine

"Voilà, la maison américaine!" explained Constance, motioning toward the split-level bungalow, its geometrical edges forming boundaries against the light. Peter looked at the combination of wooden siding, plate glass, and tapered roof; the clean lines reflected the Peugeot's headlights like sunlight to a prism, circular halos of Technicolor.

Their good-bye was efficient and non-sentimental. Constance said that she would pop the trunk and pick him up on Sunday "a 16 heur." As Peter opened the car door, Constance sighed, a prolonged sighed. She waved briefly while also trying to shake her charm bracelet toward the adhesiveness of forearm skin. Each charm held the expectation of perfection in her four daughters, a model of behaviour that left Peter walking on eggshells on the fringes of their seventeenth-century home. He was sent away to visit other local families every second weekend. This began as a forced deportation, but quickly became a welcomed retreat.

Peter tramped toward the stone walkway trying to loop the straps of his backpack over both shoulders. As Constance spun the wheels of the Peugeot in the loose gravel, he turned to wave good-bye, but the tail lights were already distant red eyes in the forest.

He hesitated at the sliding door, staring at his reflection in the plate glass. Shadowy figures moved about, but they were nowhere near the door. This was his opportunity to momentarily compose a new version of himself. He ran his fingers through his dirty- blonde hair; it was starting to grow out, but it would take awhile for the natural curls to grow back. This gesture heightened Peter's self-awareness. He was at some threshold, and these initial encounters were split second exchanges that enabled Peter to fabricate strengths and hide imperfections — a liberating but ultimately exhausting process. He had to decide quickly what persona to embrace this weekend before first contact. He placed his hands in the pockets of his threadbare cords and played with the loose strands of fabric that lined the inside of his left pocket. The vintage lime green sweat shirt inscribed with the pedigree of some Atlantic Canadian University dictated partially what Peter wanted so much to become, an independent freshmen rather than a homesick exchange student. His grungy attire only accentuated an image of maturity that did not fit in with the pressed jeans and clean lines of his new peers. The seconds were slipping away. He whispered to himself "to be somebody that matters." The lure of two temporary host brothers sanctioned the safety of comfortable pleasantries, behaviour reserved for elderly couples or host sisters; it was "total engagement" or nothing else this time around. With that decided, Peter released his hands from his pockets.

This was the first patio door that Peter had seen since he had arrived in France, but it was peculiarly the only distinguishable main entrance to the house besides the plaque that spelt out Galibault in tiles of various sizes and shades of deep blue. The letters intensified into a cobalt crescendo at the base of the "t". As Peter reminded himself that the "t" is silent in French, Sebastien appeared behind the sliding door, hands pressed against the plate glass, the moisture producing luminous handprints. His long fingers spilt over the handle in an even more awkward nervousness than Peter's own. As the sliding door slid into its mirror image, Sebastien introduced himself by thrusting his hand into Peter's, and Peter immediately assumed that this young man played an instrument—piano keys for digits that sent melodious vibrations into the fault lines of Peter's cords.

*

He and Sebastien had made their way into the living room, which consisted of stepping down two shagged carpeted steps, while his parents cleaned up after dinner. Peter did not know exactly how to start a conversation. This was the first time they had been alone together since his arrival.

They had a billiards table on a raised section of the living room, but that was not what grabbed Peter's attention first. On the wall mounted under a light was a matted photo of Sebastien in his white confirmation robe and his older brother, Serge, in a grey tuxedo with a red bowtie. They looked devilishly angelic holding wooden rosaries while staring down at the white ball on the red velvet table. Peter was reminded, momentarily, of the feel-good Jesus of his Sunday school upbringing, a sharp contrast to the emaciated Christ hanging over the pulpit at L'Église Saint-Pierre. Sebastien started fishing balls out of the pockets of the table while Peter kept staring at the photograph.

"Serge composes electronic music in Nantes" Sebastian explained noticing Peter's desire for a family history. "He usually plays clubs in the city, but he can no longer afford a proper recording space."

"That's cool" replied Peter. "I have heard that raves and dance music are quite popular here." Peter himself had never been to a rave in his entire life, but he had just finishing reading a titillating exposé on rave culture in the UK.

"I don't like the term 'dance music'; it is too mindless and that is what Serge detests about the underground music scene" said Sebastien. "It can be very unforgiving. He has had a hard go of it. The scenes change too quickly for his liking. He is a perfectionist and a minimalist, and his down tempo style went out of favour in 1992, so he has moved back home and works for Dad."

Peter was impressed and terrified by Sebastien's abrupt honesty. He had shared so much of himself, and Peter did not know what to give back — a sympathetic gaze could suggest understanding or detached indifference. They stood facing each other over the billiards table while Peter looked up at the portrait, running scenarios through his head. He was as indecisive as the moustache above Serge's upper lip, not even the grainy quality of the finish obscured its adolescent awkwardness.

Sebastien noticed the lull, and he did not want to linger too long on his sad brother, so he took his finger and tapped his left temple while smiling: "It is 'listening music'; the dancing takes place in your head." Peter looked down and met Sebastien's grinning smile.

"Do you play?" asked Sebastien. Peter noticed his dark blue eyes were offset by his olive complexion and shaggy black hair. He wore a white t-shirt and black jeans and had shed the black v-neck sweater at dinner.

"A little, but it has been awhile," said Peter, knowing full well that billiards was the one sport that did not pose too much of a threat of physical failure. Sebastien arranged the multi-coloured balls into the triangle and shuffled them into order a few times.

"The cues are in the corner…Do you want to break?"

Peter grabbed two cues and handed the longest cue to Sebastien. He placed the white ball on the small leather patch on the table. The only thing that Peter could think of was not to mess up the shot. He remembered that for a better aim, it was easier to place the cue between your knuckles. With all the force of his inner mechanics, Peter pulled back his left arm and shoulder and positioned his gaze toward the solid purple ball that was staring him down the table. Something was wrong the minute he released the tension, a momentary sense of doubt threw a kink into the image he wanted to create for himself, and with that, the cue lost its momentum.

"*Fuck,*" Peter mouthed as his palms became sweaty and the white ball slowly made contact with the purple ball at the apex of the triangle. The force moved the entire group of balls back an inch, but none of them separated.

"Go again" said Sebastien reassuringly. "Try putting the cue between your fingers."

"Ok," replied Peter sheepishly as he once again took the furtive position in front of the white ball, but not before he took off his lime green sweat shirt. He was wearing a faded soft cotton t-shirt with Bruce Springsteen on the front. This time he remained focused and took Sebastien's advice.

"Not a bad shot." The white ball broke the base of the triangle and sent several solid coloured balls rolling along the western side of the table.

"Are you a big fan of the Boss?" asked Sebastien as he prepared to sink the seven-ball.

"No, I bought the t-shirt used last year…I just liked the look and feel of it," explained Peter.

"You have a rugby player's shoulders; you must play, non?"

"Not really." Peter had secretly been doing push-ups and crunches in his cloistered room since his arrival in France four mouths ago.

"American football, then?" continued Sebastien.

"It is just in my genes, I guess" answered Peter. "They call me the *Viking* at the Lycée."

"You do have a hint of red in your stubble," laughed Sebastien. "I'd better tell Eva to hide the silverware."

Sebastien leaned over the pool table and took aim at the left corner pocket. His white t-shirt lifted up just enough to expose the tufts of black hair that trailed their way northward and southward from his bellybutton. Peter could not look away; this small piece of flesh was bordered by white cotton and a black leather belt, but it was the silver silhouette of *Tintin* on the buckle that confused and excited Peter. It was as if the childhood cartoon crush of his French Immersion upbringing had always belonged at the midriff of this nineteen year old man. Sebastien effortlessly sunk the purple ball into the left corner pocket. The next shot was easy because the white ball was lined up with the ten-ball along the rim of the table, but Sebastien wasn't concentrating. He hit the ball with too much force, and the ten-ball bounced off the plastic lining of the pocket.

"Merde!" shouted Sebastien, swinging his arms to the top of his head. "You have caught me off guard. You are striped, so I would aim for the nine-ball if I were you."

"I used to read *Tintin*" Peter said, wanting Sebastien to acknowledge what he had seen.

"I still read *Tintin*" said Sebastien, as he tucked his t-shirt into the front of his pants and exposed the glistening stylized, erect bangs of this eternally adolescent sleuth. "I have always had a strange thought about Tintin and his relationships." Sebastien went on to move his right arm under his t-shirt to scratch at an imaginary itch at the base of his left nipple. This left Peter with a full-frontal view of the silvery *Tintin*.

"What kind of strange thought?" asked Peter while trying to set up his next shot.

"I think on some subconscious level that Tintin totally wants to fuck Capitaine Haddock."

"What?" Peter gulped. He had dropped out of his crouch and gripped the cue between both of his hands. He had never imagined Tintin making love to the gruff captain. His fantasies involved Tintin exploring the bodies of nameless characters that coloured the landscape.

"It's like this," explained Sebastien. "Captaine Haddock parades around his masculinity in a campy uniform, and *you* know that Tintin is secretly getting off staring at the Captaine's ass while stumbling over drunk or in free-fall."

"I need proof." Peter returned to the billiard's table. "I'm calling the twelve-ball in the right corner," he said as an afterthought.

"How about the scene from *Le Crabe aux pinces d'or* where the Capitaine drunkenly transforms Tintin into a bubbling bottle of champagne — it gives new meaning to popping the cork, doesn't it?"

Peter had come undone; he wasn't prepared for such specifics. All he needed to do was finish the shot, but all he could picture was Sebastien swimming in champagne. The cue felt heavy in his hands, so he gripped it tighter.

"You are crazy" replied Peter as the twelve-ball disappeared into the pocket.

"No I am not! Trust me. There has been stranger things suggested about Tintin; I mean come on! His best friend is a Wire Fox Terrier."

"What is this talk of Tintin?" echoed a voice from the dinning room.

Their game was cut short as Madame Galibault brought down the disgestifs, a tray of coffee and four cognac glasses. After several months in France, Peter became accustomed to the various drinking glasses and the sharp bite of their multi-coloured liquids. It was Monsieur Galibault who brought down the bottle of cognac. He was a stout man with a loud moustache and perfectly combed haired. This was the first host father figure that Peter had seen who wore jeans.

Madame Galibault wore a red and gold scarf tied in her long black hair with black slacks and a white top. She was elegantly, but casually put together. She was a whole foot taller than her husband, and she wore her height well. Peter though to himself that they looked like a French version of *Sonny and Cher*, and they endorsed a lifestyle of Pastisse and pop-psychology in the early evening.

Everybody took their seats in the living room, Monsieur and Madame Galibault on the couch, Sebastien on the foot stool and Peter on an old wooden chair that's worn frame creaked each time Peter moved a muscle. There was a large bronze serving tray that shined like exaggerated treasure in a pirate movie in the centre of the room adorned with candles, magazines, and tiled coasters. There was barely enough room for the coffee and cognac. It all elaborately sat on top of a brown trunk that separated the room and the party into two groups.

"A notre jeune canadien," toasted Monsieur Galibault. Peter lifted his glass and sipped at the bitter-sweet alcohol. Sebastien downed his cognac in one gulp and quickly moved to the coffee, his parents following suit. While they were adding crystallized cubes of dark sugar to their espresso cups, Peter brought out his collection of relics from home.

It was tradition of Peter to give a formal lecture about all his friends back home to his new hosts. This took roughly an hour and finished with the displaying all of his graduation photos and yearbook on the table and translating a few key entries. On this occasion, after dinner drinks seemed like the only appropriate time to bring up such personal things. If he delayed any longer, he would feel uncomfortable bringing them up later on in the weekend.

"All your friends are *minion* Pierre," winked Monsieur Galibault. Peter's friends back home were mostly female students from his enriched English class, and they had all given him personally inscribed photos. Monsieur Galibault went on to organize the photos into distinct groups, pinpointing the racial origins of Hillsborough High's graduation class. He stumbled with Ruchi's photograph defining her somewhere between Spanish and North African.

"Eva, where would you place her? Tangiers or Sevilla?" exclaimed Monsieur Galibault as he waved a wallet size photo over his head.

"She looks more like she is from the Western Sahara," answered Madame Galibault. "Let me see the next one!"

They effortlessly moved to the next photo, not even bothering to look at the inscriptions on the back. Peter had lost control, and he caught Sebastien leafing through his yearbook with a curiosity that could have passed as wonder or pity. He lifted his head from the page and looked at Peter with a tender expression. "You have a lot of signatures...must be popular back home?"

Peter couldn't answer; he just nodded while trying to hurry the exposition along. He wanted nothing more than to be alone with

Sebastien, and the yearbook posed an embarrassing obstacle to such a desire. Sebastien stopped on page fifty-six and read the short personalized inscription under Peter's graduation photo which memorialized a frozen stare obscured by blonde curls. "Heard Melodies Are Sweet, But Those Unheard Are Sweeter; Therefore, Ye soft pipes, Play On." Peter glanced again at Sebastien wondering if he felt as "unravished" as he did.

He quickly gathered all of his relics of homesickness except for the yearbook that Sebastien still gleamed over like an illuminated text. All the signatures and catch phrases danced around the edges of the honour roll. The moment that he met Sebastien's eyes over the ritual naming of missed friends, something snapped inside Peter's fragile frame of reference. It was as if he was observing himself from a new vantage point, a space of possibility. In this imagined future state, that was not a university campus, Peter couldn't help but notice the neediness of his behaviour, for he knew he did not really miss his old life as much as he feared a new one.

"Pierre come here and see my mosaic," beckoned Monsieur Galibault suddenly. "My parents' house in Mauritania had mosaics in a cloistered courtyard. I have never forgotten reading under the old fig tree as all the blue and yellow swirls in the thousands of tiles lifted my spirits. It was hard spending so much time alone."

Madame Galibault had a stack of four chipped plates. She had inherited the Seir Breur stoneware with the topaz blue "petit Breton" figures in their traditional costumes from her great aunt in Bretagne. Next to the stack was a shoebox of broken ceramic pieces. The black bird was the only part of the mosaic complete within the wooden framed tray.

"According to the medieval bestiary, the black bird is the incarnation of desire in flight. Its melodies soothe and excite the mind at the same time," lectured Sebastien teasingly from across the room. "The truly devout did not approve of these birds' sweet songs, but they nonetheless kept them in cages all the while inflicting pain on their flesh for such transgression."

"That's horrid," blurted Madame Galibault with a slight laugh and not taking her eyes off her work. "I always start in the centre and work my way out. I used a teapot to form the bird; black is such a hard colour to find in great quantity."

Peter remained standing over the table while Madame Galibault kept turning a rectangular piece of ceramic into different positions, looking for the perfect fit.

"Poor Mme. Hourdeau would be rolling in her grave if she could see her dishes" quipped Monsieur Galibault from the couch.

"Mais, Jacques, they're chipped!" yelled Madame Galibault in a quick, short voice that froze the minute it was perceived by human ears. Peter was startled by the sudden intensity in the room. Sebastien went back to the yearbook, leaving Peter in the firing line. He kept replaying the past several minutes in his head trying to determine when the mine field had been set. This was when being an exchange student posed it most dangerous challenge. Peter moved in to inspect the mosaic more closely.

Monsieur Galibault had turned on the TV and did not give his wife the satisfaction of a response; he sat back on the light brown leather couch, his form regained some of its joy as it made crinkling noises until he was completely settled for the evening. The news flashed school blockades and security guards.

"It is absurd all these precautions. Who are they trying to keep out, striking civil servants or Algerian terrorists?!" miffed Madame Galibault. She was proud of her statement and waited for a rebuttal from her husband.

"On s'arrête Eva," pleaded Monsieur Galibault. "Comments like that will not be tolerated here or in the office".

"Nous sommes tous les étrangers," whispered Madame Galibault under her breath as she moved herself and her cognac to the couch. She had been lulled to a ceasefire by the worry in her husband's eyes. Peter took her seat at the work station and read the black tiles like brail. The smooth surface and rough groves eased Peter out of an awkward situation.

Sebastien got up, stretched. He yawned while clasping his fingers around the yearbook well above his head. He was all arms and hands, and he rushed toward Peter with an exaggerated stride. All of a sudden, his lanky arms and delicate hands were on Peter's shoulder working out the remaining tension. Peter unclasped his feet that were neatly tucked behind his chair as Sebastien bent down and whispered in his ear. "You should've never cut your hair." Sebastien's warm breath slipped into the fabric of Peter's clothes, mingling with the sweat that was settling on Peter's pale white chest.

"You need to hear me play," said Sebastien. "Let's go upstairs."

The blackbird's wings in the mosaic glistened with Peter's fingerprints as both young men left to go upstairs. Monsieur and Madame Galibault cuddled on the couch waiting for the evening to end.

"Bon nuit, les garçons," echoed through the living room, up the stairs and into the bedroom.

SWEAT

Barry Webster

Sweat

My body was changing. This happens to girls my age, so I was not surprised. In health class I'd learned how our breasts will swell, our hipbones billow sideways and hair patches appear along the hidden valleys of our bodies. I expected everything and, despite Mother's warnings, revelled in the sudden flesh coating my bones, the rounding-out of what had formerly been level.

One thing I did not expect — and that I couldn't stand — was the stickiness. A glue-like residue veneered my armpits, the tips of my breasts and the space between my legs. It was clammy and viscous. It made my thighs stick together and my arms adhere to my torso. My toes melded into one solid, beak-like protuberance. I perspired daily but I did not perspire as other thirteen-year-old girls did for, you see, *I sweat honey*.

This is not a metaphor but true life. From my pores came liquid, golden honey such as the bees crave, such as Father puts on his toast every morning before he slices it into strips.

"Tests show your perspiration has the normal levels of sodium and chloride," said Doctor Merton, Cartwright's resident physician, his voice even, "but it has unusually high levels of sugar making its composition similar to —" he gulped "— bee-honey."

At home Mother removed my clothes and coated me with sea salt, driftwood shavings, baking soda, talcum powder, coral dust — anything to staunch the flow. She forbade me to eat corn syrup, caramel squares or jujubes and she uprooted all the flowers in our garden fearing they'd attract bees (though bees hadn't been seen in this part of Labrador for decades — the only thing here is rock stained with seasalt.) One night she snuck into our neighbour's yard and gutted their tiny flowerbed. "I don't know who did it," she said into the phone the next morning. Mother even drove me to Mary's Harbour to get a second opinion, but the doctor there agreed with the first. "Your perspiration has the standard level of protein and fatty acids but there's all this unmetabolized sugar. I've never seen anything like it!"

Mother threatened to leave Labrador to get help. Our town was similar to many of the other towns along the shore; it was charming but hemmed in and not exactly known for outstanding medicine. Cartwright was always full of the smell of bonfires and rotting flounder, the cry of seagulls and the thump of wood hitting the earth. Fishermen shuffled their feet along the seaweed-strewn boards of the once-busy port. And wind blew everywhere, wailing up one street and down another; it rattled our windows at night, splattered bugs on the walls of the new steel foundry and whipped telephone wires. I'd always feared the Cartwright wind, but lately I found myself fleeing our clapboard house just to run into it. Some things are greater than fear. I wanted to know what they were.

Every night, doing my homework, I felt honey-drops crawl down my neck, beading in the small of my back, collecting in the creases around my waist. Honey seeped through my hair, darkened the fabric of my cotton pinafores. Each time Mother threw my clothes in the washer, the rotating pivot got clogged and the machine stopped running. I showered three times a day, watching the water chase honey globs down the drain along with things that had gotten trapped on me — dust, fallen hairs, fruit flies. It didn't take long for my sweat to block the pipes in the basement. Again and again, Father had to phone the plumber.

School, however, was the worst. When classes started in September I thought I could hide my affliction, but Mr. Schmidt soon noticed syrup beads clinging to my forehead. "Sue, are you feeling ill? Do you want to go home?" Whenever I raised my hand, my arm made a loud *fffffflit* and everyone turned toward me. One day, when I flung back my hair, a globule flew off and landed on the open textbook of Estelle Beaverbank. Estelle had a mountain of blond hair lacquered into a series of curlicues and a slot-like mouth you wanted to slip nickels into. "Ooo, gross," she said. "Sue's a filthy glue-girl!"

The boys got in the habit of inviting me to hang out with them at the end of the school day. I'd usually escape down the alley beside the portables, but one Friday, curious to see what would happen, I shrugged and followed. For a minute, I thought I was being led to the bushes — a spot at the end of the football field where people hung out or "got friendly" or both — but they turned the opposite way, towards a large oak tree. We sat in a circle on the shaded grass while the boys eyed me solemnly. No one spoke. The sun hung high in the sky; a dragonfly circled my forehead. Then, the boys dared each other to touch me. I studied my legs draped in wrinkled trousers that resembled their own. Their behaviour confused me; I felt embarrassed without knowing why.

"Put your finger on the drop on the end of her chin and put it in your mouth. Here's two bucks you won't."

"Touch her kneecap and lick it. If you do, I'm the one who steals cigs from Variety Plus tonight."

"Ten bucks if you put your tongue in her ear; there's a whole pool full inside."

None of them touched me. They stared at a honey-drop clinging to the end of my bent elbow. As they waited for it to drop, their faces stopped twitching, their eyes darkened and they became stone-still. One boy accidentally got some on his hand but didn't put it in his mouth. When he got up to go home — it was dinnertime by then — he just wiped it on the grass and sauntered off, trying to look courageous.

*

My downfall began the day Jimmy Bridock asked me out on a date. Jimmy smelled like wood fires, smoked venison, and gunpowder. He had a cowlick that swung on his forehead like a horse's tail batting imaginary flies. His round cheeks were volcanic with acne. He had blue, moist-looking eyes and his cracked lips were always twisting one way, then another, as if chronically unsure what expression to take. He'd always had an interest in me. When I'd push open the door of the girl's washroom, he'd often be standing in the hall with his head down. When I walked past him, he'd look away and kick at the floor — but if I turned back, I'd see him squinting after me.

That was last year. Now, in grade eight, with my sweat flowing, Jimmy became bolder. In shop class, I was hammering parallel-placed nails into a wood beam. Unlike the other students, even the boys, I could whack the silver heads straight on so the iron rods thrust in without bending. Jimmy eyed my forearm moving up and down. In the silent space between blows, Jimmy spoke to me for the first time ever. His voice started as a rumbling in his throat and emerged as a gasp, then a strange sing-song squeaking as his thick tongue stumbled around the syllables. Did he speak so rarely that when he did, he used tools rusted from lack of use?

"You're stronger than other girls," he rasped. A cloud of sawdust hung in the air between us. A power drill wailed. "If we had an arm-wrestle," his voice rose triumphantly over the din, "I bet you'd win."

The room was now full of the repetitive rah-rah sound of saws cutting. I raised my head. Jimmy had kind eyes. The swath of protruding, unshaven hairs across his jaw was like a fire-razed forest. He seemed innocent, more standoffish than the rest, and so I trusted him. He smiled a checkerboard grin, lowered his head and walked away.

The next day in the cafeteria Jimmy walked up to me and made a knock-knock sound on the tabletop with his knuckles. His eyes were wide open, blazing. When he spoke, spit flew from his lips and landed on my hamburger-macaroni. His cheeks were flushed. Was this because I'd spoken to him yesterday? Was I the first girl who hadn't run away from him in terror?

He said, "If you don't mind it, we can get together after school. I want to go to the bushes."

Jimmy's smile wavered, disappeared, struggled to reform, slanted sideways, collapsed, reformed — I answered, "Yes," like I said when the boys asked me to the end of the field. The word gave me a feeling of what I thought was power.

Jimmy's cowlick trembled like a radar device. His lips parted, spread, lifted and his smile was so huge I could see the line separating his teeth from his gums. White and pink. A flag. "Great," he said. "Let's meet by the bleachers at four."

We stood facing each other. I stared past him for a very long time. Somewhere in the distance I sensed winds lashing against seaside cliffs. If I found and gave way to a desire for Jimmy, would a balance be regained? Would my honey finally stop flowing?

*

Cartwright was playing the visiting Dove Brook and we were winning. I met Jimmy in the striped shade behind the crowded football stands; above us, everyone had gathered to cheer. I could see the bushes from here, like three ice-cream scoops near the huge, stiff oak that the other boys were so fond of.

"Way to go, Cartwright. Way to go!" *Clap clap.*

Jimmy leaned against a wood pillar and fidgeted as if his entire body were itchy. Immediately he said, "Let's walk by the stands."

The football players were running two abreast in zigzag formations. A squad of cheerleaders in yellow shirts and red skirts (I recognized Estelle among them) shook pom-poms and screamed.

"Cart-wright is all-right! Cart-wright can fight-fight!" *Clap clap.*

Jimmy beamed as if they were cheering for him. He stopped and turned a couple of times toward the crowd so people could see his face. I wondered if we'd come this route so he could be seen going into the bushes with a girl. Was this his way of raising his status amongst the boys? If it was, I didn't mind. I might have considered using him for the same purpose. The boys by the oak tree always fled after sitting with me and I had to walk home alone. I'd never had friends at school. Even before my honey problem, my muscles and plaid shirts frightened people. I looked at Jimmy's pants, plaid with intersecting lines that wavered as he walked. As we approached the wall of bracken, I became frightened. What are we actually going to do in there? Jimmy motioned for me to sit on the stone-bumpy, shadow-dappled earth, and I reminded myself that I was stronger than him.

Jimmy shyly asked me if he could wipe his finger along my collarbone. I nodded. He wanted a honey drop from the hollow below my ankle and I said yes. He asked for some sweetness from the space between my breasts, just visible in the V-cut of my shirt. I let him have that too. As he peered at the golden thread hanging from his fingertip, I wondered if I could make myself like a boy. It was probably interesting to want — *really* want — another person. How fascinating and unusual it'd be to find someone attractive and completely enjoy his or her presence.

A wind blew that rattled the tree branches and brought the scent of faraway forests, pine sap, juniper flowers — a scent part piquant, part sour. The wind woke an excitement in my motionless body. It made every pore in my skin open wide and caused my backbone to straighten so completely that I was sitting more erect than I'd ever done in my life. The mouths of my ears gaped and my eardrums became as still as the water on a lake so distant and hidden that no wind had ever rippled its surface; a lake that had waited an eternity for something even remotely resembling weather.

What was I listening for?

To my surprise, Jimmy brought the honeyed fingers of his hand together and shoved them into his mouth. His large tongue swirled out and round in a long, luxuriant movement licking the honey off both sides of his fingers. Honey drops glimmered on his lips. He stared me straight in the eyes as he loudly and definitively swallowed. His Adam's apple leapt briefly forward, as if a small man imprisoned in his neck struck a fist against his throat.

A strange expression came over Jimmy's face. His cheeks slowly reddened and his eyes grew larger, bulging forward like egg yolks.

His chest had stopped moving.

"Jimmy?" I said. "Jimmy? Are you all right?"

Flapping his hands in the air, he raced out of the trembling bushes just in time for the home team to score its final field goal. The spiralling football descended through the posts and struck him square in the face. He fell to the earth and, mouth gaping, thrashed on the ground like a fish pulled from water.

I charged out into the blinding sunshine.

The spectators in the stands turned toward me. "Dr. Merton!" I cried. "Somebody call Dr. Merton!"

When the ambulance arrived, everyone was on the field shaking hands with the winning players. Only Estelle noticed me, her shaggy pom-pom fronds dangling from her hands like tentacles. She eyed me for what seemed like an eternity, her head a stuck weathercock. On the front of her cheerleader uniform, below her right breast, a circle of sweat bloomed like a flower.

Jimmy remained in the hospital all night.

*

The next morning I learned that my honey had caused the sides of Jimmy's throat to adhere. Though he recovered, his desk remained empty for a month. This wasn't altogether unusual. I assumed he was in the woods helping his father cut open metal traps. It was October now; the hunting season was in full swing.

But still, other students grew wary of me. After Jimmy's disappearance, the boys didn't ask me to be part of their after-school circle. When students came upon drops of honey on the school steps or on the handle of the water fountain, they regarded them first with annoyance, then outrage and finally with pure, unmitigated terror. In gym class no one let me join their squads. Exasperated, Mr. Schmidt said, "Kids you can sit beside Sue. She won't bite."

I noticed Estelle everywhere. She was constantly talking, her voice no longer high-pitched and metallic, but husky, full of sly hissing s's and cruel, explosive p's and t's. She spoke at an agonizingly low decibel that everyone seemed to hear but me. And she listened to people, one hand on her chin, mentally storing this bit of gossip and that bit of truth. She'd become a seamstress stitching together the rumours and facts that were bandied about. From myriad ingredients, she created a seamless cloth woven together with real needs and deeply-rooted desire. In the end the story was not hers but everyone's.

Everyone but me, that is. My new isolation did not trouble me as much as hearing my name whispered everywhere and not knowing what that meant. I stared into the washroom mirror. Behind me were the reflected, beige cubicle doors, like a row of pale-faced sentinels, about which sounded a diabolical hiss. "Sssue, Ssssue, Ssssssue, Sssssssue." The sound joined to other words or half-words, or verbs without objects or objects without verbs or lone, great big juicy adjectives.

"Piggy-girl, Piiiiig!"

"It's because of her condition…"

"…it was bound to happen…"

"…she wooed Jimmy into the bushes…"

"…stripped him down…"

"…and the catastrophe happened!"

I still couldn't find the through-line to these shattered sentences which, pasted together, now formed the story of my life.

"What catastrophe?" I cried. The hissing stopped and the beige sentinels stared. Before me a lone, silver tap dripped once into the sink.

Sometimes I'd overhear a refreshing, "This stuff about Sue Masonty is ridiculous," but that was rare.

At last, after a week of conjecturing, I was able to put the disparate pieces of the tale into a whole. I was wandering, head down, through the school parking lot after school. I entered the field where boys were playing flag football and, when I stepped onto the burnt wood of the bleachers, heard my name spoken. All the boys had stopped playing and they crowded together, facing me in a tight, protective knot. From some hands hung crepe streamers. Since Jimmy's injury, the boys were forced to play flag football, not the real rough-and-tumble version, as everyone was now more keenly aware of the fragility of the male body.

I heard a player say, "Don't let her get near us or we'll have to saw ours off too."

The wind had partly ripped one boy's streamer and he knelt, sobbing, cradling it in his hands.

It was then that everything fell together in my mind. The story went like this: Jimmy and I crawled into the space beneath the bushes and proceeded to make love. But when he entered me, he got stuck and couldn't get out. The rumour mill had produced two endings. In one, he had to saw his penis off at the root to get free of me and, full of shame, fled into the forest and was now wandering bloodied and penis-less about the rocks of Labrador. In the other version he was absorbed by me completely and was now crouched suffocating somewhere amongst the twists and turns of my Fallopian tubes.

But didn't anyone see him run fully membered from the bushes? I recalled he was lying face-down, and most people were fixated on the rotating ball as it descended through the goalposts. No one cared what happened to it once it crossed the line. Only Estelle had watched me, so the story was hers.

The boys huddled together, their flimsy flags fluttering. The kneeling boy wept bitterly into his torn streamer. He turned towards me and shouted, "Bitch!" He then picked a stone and threw it. The rock bounced off the bench in front of me.

"I didn't do anything!" I cried. The other boys crouched and snatched stones from the earth and flung them in my direction. One struck me in the shin; another cut the side of my cheek.

I turned and ran from the field, crying uncontrollably, and when I reached the street, continued running southward. The pounding of my feet on the gravel echoed about the silent clapboard houses that marched past me in jerky, disjointed steps. Women on porches flapped tea-towels like striped whips, and barking dogs thrashed on leashes taut as tightropes. Rows of fence-pickets pointed skyward like white knives. The earth was gouged, cratered and gashed as if hacked with a huge dagger. I passed a man pulling a buggy joined to his waist with a rope knotted thick as veins; a lady stepped from the white-walled Catholic church, the sides of her hat rim flapping like oars. Down one street I charged and then up another, criss-crossing Cartwright's checkerboard pattern. The air smelled of sea salt, tar, decaying scallops, motor oil.

When I reached the open field near my parents' house, I stopped running and stood panting on the empty plain. The wind struck me square in the face, whipped the bangs off my forehead, fluttered my eyelashes and dried the spittle on my lips. I looked down at my body: this body I lived in, this body I carted about wherever I went. These carbuncled fingers, these bulging thighs, this chest rising and falling like the swell of the ocean were mine — were me.

It was then I knew: air will free me. The wind I once feared will lift me high above the earth-bound people of Cartwright. Wind is what happens when air falls in love with itself. I'll love the sweetness of sweat and it will dissolve rocks hurled like missiles at my head. I spread my arms wide to the howling gale that shot into my open pores, roared through my body like Niagara, as a shower of glistening honey drops fell like manna onto the parched stony earth.

EVA

Zsolt Alapi

EVA

The boy sat on the large drift log watching his father chopping the onions and cubing the meat to be added to the stew. Behind them, the vast lake stretched far beyond where the eye could see, its waves striking the shore and leaving the scum of white foam, dead fish, shells, and gull feathers.

The beach they were on was a long, deserted span and they had come here to spend the day and cook the traditional gulyás, a Hungarian meat stew, over the open cauldron suspended from two forked pieces of driftwood that his father had skillfully fashioned for the purpose. The boy watched his father place the onions and cubes of beef into the sizzling fat and smelled the pungent odor that brought the saliva running into his mouth. He watched the sinews of his father's arms as he stoked the flames and saw the roll of flesh, the first hint of old man's flab, protrude between the umbilicus and the groin, the sheer cloth of his bathing suit and the short, strong legs that were hairless from the knees down because of the years of wearing high, cheap cotton leggings.

"Tell your sister to come here, Stephen; be quick about it," his father said. Stephen ran down the beach to where his sister sat sketching a dead tree protruding along the water line.

"That's good," Stephen said, and stood for a while admiring the half-finished charcoal etching. Then: "Father says to come...now, right away," he added, his voice rising.

She folded her pad and replaced the charcoal pencil neatly into its kit and followed him wordlessly back to the fire.

"Watch this food carefully," their father said to her. "Make sure it doesn't burn and add water and stir it...you know how. I'm going into the village to buy Eva some soft drinks; she finds the lemonade too sour. I'll be back as soon as I can." The village, they knew, was a good half an hour's walk away.

He put on his shirt over his swimsuit and walked off, then halted. "You, Stephen. Swim out to see how Eva is doing on the float. See if she needs anything...some sunscreen or something. The sun is very strong today." He walked on, stooped, toward the main road.

Stephen was a strong swimmer for his age. His father had taught the children to swim when Stephen was six and his sister eight. He had done this by throwing them into the creek after having explained the rudiments of the "dog-paddle". As he swam toward the figure lying on the rubber float about a half a mile from the shore, Stephen remembered the way the cold creek water had felt then, remembered his own fear and desperate attempt to keep his head above water, all the while gasping for breath while his father's stern gray eyes watched him from the shore. He had finally reached it after a struggle and found that he could swim then, and he had told this to his father proudly, after the initial terror, through chattering teeth. But his father had turned away to fling his sister into the water.

Stephen remembered this as he swam in a slow measured breast stroke and heard again his sister's scream and saw the fear in her milk-blue eyes as she went down again and again, screaming, then gasping until his father finally plunged in and pulled her out and roughly tossed her, coughing, onto the coarse grass. As Stephen thought of this, he felt a cold current sweep over his torso and felt his groin contract and the flesh raise all over his body.

Then, he was by the rubber raft. The young woman was lying belly down on it, her eyes closed, one hand trailing in the water. She wore a tight-fitting, one-piece, red bathing suit whose neck straps had been loosened for an even tan. They drifted next to her hands in the water.

Stephen looked at her carefully ringleted hair and the thin lips that seemed to pout even at rest as his eyes followed the outline of her body from the honey-brown shoulders down to the end of the red suit that curved around the tight furrow of her buttocks. She was beautiful, he thought, and he spoke her name softly:

"Eva."

Nothing

"Eva." Again, then louder. "Father wants to know if you need anything. He's gone into town to get you some pop. Well…?" He stopped, a catch in his voice.

Eva opened her eyes slowly, languorously. She fixed him in her stare, measuring his head as he trod water near her.

"Come here, Stephen. Here. On the raft." She spoke coldly, used to giving orders and being obeyed.

Stephen did as she said and climbed onto the raft, almost tipping her over in the process. The water invaded the sausage-like rubber tubing, wetting her suit until she too sat up. Now they were both sitting, balancing, facing each other. Stephen noticed the top of her smooth, full breasts protruding above the line of the bathing suit. He turned red and cast his eyes down toward the water gathering in small pools around his own groin, feeling the painful swelling of his sex constricted by his swim trunks.

Eva looked down at him mockingly, then leaned toward him, grabbing his thin shoulders to steady herself. As she did this, her breasts brushed softly against his arms and chest. He smelled her distinct odor, the sweat of her body mingled with faint traces of Noxema, sunscreen, and the algae and fish smell of the lake's water.

She reached behind her and produced a small tube of the suntan lotion.

"Rub this on me; the arms and shoulders first."

Stephen did as he was told, his excitement growing with his embarrassment.

"Now the neck and chest area. Do it," she said, her voice rising impatiently. His hands trailed down from the collar-bone to touch the golden skin of her breasts, feeling their softness. He felt as if he were in a trance and shuddered as she ran the long, red lacquered nail of her index finger over the taut acrylic of his trunks, over his hard stem, making it twitch involuntarily. She smiled at him wickedly:

"Does that feel good? What is that thing, little boy? It's so hard...what would you like to do with it?" she said, giving it a painful tug.

Stephen felt too far gone to answer. His hand reached lower into the top of her swimsuit, encircling each breast, kneading them, feeling the hard nipples pressed against his wet palms.

Then, she suddenly slapped him hard. She grabbed both of his hands firmly and held them level with her face. She glared at him, her voice like ice:

"What do you think you're doing, you dirty little monkey? Who do you think you are, touching me? Get off this raft right now! Now, I said!" She pushed him hard and he tumbled backwards into the water.

When Stephen surfaced, she was lying on her back, her eyes closed, the straps of her suit done chastely up around her neck. He trod water, not daring to address her. After about ten minutes, she was still silent, immobile, so he swam closer and murmured:

"Eva...?"

No answer.

"Eva....?: he swallowed, "I'm sorry...Eva....please..."

She opened her eyes and smiled at him.

"For what, you silly boy? Now, enough of this; take me out farther. You know how...push the raft down near my feet."

Stephen felt happy again. She had smiled and maybe she would love him still. His shame receded into some remote corner where it was cold and dark. He grabbed a hold of the raft's end with both hands and started to swim, using the frog kick. They moved slowly through the water.

Eva had closed her eyes and seemed to be asleep. Then, slowly, she lifted a leg up, then both, until her heels were drawn up to her buttocks. Slowly, the knees began to open and close rhythmically.

Stephen watched the area between her legs in fascination. The tight, red swimsuit had ridden up her buttocks to the point where the lower halves were almost entirely exposed. The wetness of her suit accentuated the cleft of her pubis and he saw some matted tufts of hair that protruded near where the tight Spandex material bit into the flesh. He swallowed hard.

Eva wiggled her bottom and moved closer to him, her eyes half-closed, emitting a soft moan. She let her right hand drift down the inside of her thigh and moved one long finger beneath the split of the tight material, revealing dark curls of hair and a brief glimpse of flesh.

Stephen leaned forward, mesmerized, his own breath coming in quick, short gasps. He was inches away from her, staring, smelling her strong odor, feeling his hard flesh protrude underneath the cold water. Goosebumps covered his body and he drew half of his torso onto the raft, immersing part of it under water.

Suddenly, Eva sat up, her eyes blazing with fury.

"You dirty little shit," she screamed. As she did so, the raft, half immersed because of his weight, tipped over, toppling them both into the water.

They both came up to the surface within feet of each other. Eva gasped, swallowing water, trying to find voice, her carefully constructed hairdo matted wet, eyeliner running in streams down her face. Terrified, Stephen turned toward the shore and began to swim in a rapid crawl, breathing fast at first, then more rhythmically, until he thought of nothing, only the steady, even stroke, the synchronized kicking of the legs, looking up only to gauge his distance toward his sisters who sat by the ambers of the fire.

*

Stephen threw himself down by the fire and covered himself with a large bath towel, shivering even though the sun was still hot. He smelled the food and felt hungry and wondered when they would eat. It was all he wanted to think of now. His sister looked at him curiously and arched her eyebrows in a silent question. Stephen shrugged and asked:

"When are we eating?"

"When father says so, or when she want to…you know that."

She gave the coals a stir with a charred stick. They both sat in silence looking out at the lake.

Soon, their father arrived with some cans of soft drinks. There were large, wet patches on the back of his shirt and near his armpits.

"Where's Eva," he demanded.

Stephen didn't say anything, but only pointed out toward the distant figure on the raft that seemed to be moving ever farther away from them. The father checked the stew and then began pacing nervously up and down the sand while periodically checking his watch. Finally, Stephen went up to him and said:

"I'm hungry. When can we eat? When will supper be ready?"

"When Eva comes, and only then. Did you go out to see her like I told you to? Did you do anything to offend her?" His father spoke quickly, drawing deeply on a cigarette. Stephen felt something hollow in his stomach and stammered:

"We tipped the raft, but it was an accident. I'm sure she knows that." His father cast a withering glance at him and sighed deeply. Then, he took off his shirt, stubbed out his cigarette, and plunged into the water and began swimming out toward the raft in slow, measured strokes.

Stephen and his sister sat, watching. They saw their father reach the raft and lean on the end. He stayed there for a long time.

Meanwhile, the two children started opening a loaf of the pumpernickel and began dipping hunks of bread into the boiling stew. Stephen had already eaten four pieces, but he was getting hungrier with each mouthful. Finally, he turned to his sister and said:

"I'm eating. I can't wait any more."

"Don't Stephen. Please."

"Then I'm going to swim out there to see what's going on."

"Suit yourself."

He entered the water and began to swim in a strong, rapid crawl, stopping every now and then to gauge his distance to the raft. It seemed very far. Just over half way there he switched to a slow breaststroke and began to get very tired. For the first time, he felt afraid of the water, feeling the cold currents strike his body and the steady waves push foam and tufts of algae into his face and extended arms. At one point, he felt his hands touch something cold and soft and saw the large, bloated carcass of a dead carp floating belly up near him. He swam rapidly away, gritting his teeth in revulsion and holding his lips tightly pressed together so he would not accidentally swallow some of the water where the fish had been.

His lungs began to burn from the effort and the muscles in his neck and shoulders were aching from holding his head above the water. He was still maybe four hundred yards from the raft, and as he glanced back toward his sister on the beach he realized that he was perhaps a mile from the shore, farther than he had ever swam before, and a real fear of drowning assailed him.

How deep is the water here, he thought? What would it feel like to sink down into its inky depth? Did it get colder as one went deeper? And would he be wrapped in brown seaweed like the boy they had heard about last summer who had drowned and was found only six weeks after, blue, his face nearly erased by the erosion of the water. Perhaps it would be painless after the water filled your lungs. Maybe it was true that after the first minute you no longer knew if you were sinking or floating up into the night sky. And the shells were like the stars inverted in the water. Like heaven where his mother was, where she had gone, so he had been told seven years ago when he was five. But he had stopped believing that some time ago, just as he no longer believed that she was watching him from heaven. Then why did his father tell him and his sister to buy Eva a card last Mother's Day? Eva was his cousin and she was only nineteen, only she looked and acted much older, more world-wise. She smoked, and he loved to watch it come out as she exhaled through her elegant nostrils. Yes, she was a lady, Eva. She ate daintily, laughed at the right moments when his father told stories to adults, played bridge well, told his sister how to dress and comb her hair. Sometimes Eva also cried out at night, for he had heard her at those times when she entered the room where he and his father slept. She would crawl into bed with his father and they would whisper things he could never hear and then, after, he would hear the rhythmic movement of the bedsprings, Eva's soft moans, and once his own father crying out, sharply, as if in pain, then muffling the sound into his pillow. And if Eva was his cousin, why had she signed a note he had found one Christmas addressed to his father as "Your little wife," and why did she wear the antique earrings brought from the old country that had belonged to his dead mother?

And then Stephen was blubbering and coughing, feeling his father's strong arm gripping him across his chest and under his left armpit.

"What in God's name is it with you, boy?" his father was shouting. "Have you got a cramp or something? Lucky for you Eva saw you, even though she knew you must be fooling, as usual." His father sounded a bit hysterical and Stephen felt him ease his grip on his body. They were only about fifty feet from the raft.

"Lie on your back like I taught you," his father told him gruffly.

Stephen did so and felt a calm peace, felt his heartbeat slowing, felt secure again as he held onto his father's shoulders.

"I'm ok now, but I got tired from the long swim, I guess," he said, trying to smile.

"So why didn't you stay by the fire like I told you to?"

"I wanted to find out why you weren't coming back. Besides, we're both starving." His father disregarded the last statement and lowered his voice, speaking to him angrily:

"Why did you tip the float and dump Eva into the water? She's very hurt by your behavior, you know."

"But it wasn't my fault," he stammered. "Besides, she…she…" he paused, red from embarrassment and the exertion of the swim and treading water.

"I want you to apologize to Eva. Tell her you were a very stupid boy for upsetting the raft. Tell her you love her. Say 'I'm very sorry; forgive me.' Do it, Stephen. Now!"

He looked at his father, but he had turned away and was looking at Eva on the raft.

"Now, or no supper. Do it quick and then we'll push Eva back on the raft and eat. I mean it!"

They were almost by the raft now. Stephen was shivering. He was hungry, tired, and wanted to cry, but his father's icy stare showed no sympathy. He felt a cold current of water strike him, and then he approached the raft.

Eva was lying on her stomach, her head facing away from him.

"Eva…" he barely whispered her name, then, louder, "Eva…"

Slowly, she turned her head, gazing at him impassively.

"I'm……sorry."

Then, almost blinded by his tears, he saw her smile, triumphantly, but he was swimming as fast as he could toward the shore, his heart racing, the fatigue and fear gone, only the anger and shame remaining, his father's own angry cries drowned out by the splashing of the water.

*

He sat on a large drift log bleached white by the sun like the underbelly of a dead fish. Farther off, his sister knelt by the fire, occasionally stirring the cauldron with a large wooden spoon.

Eventually, his father reached the shore pushing Eva on the float before him. He stumbled awkwardly over the sand and hurriedly brought a towel to wrap around her shoulders and then lit her a cigarette. Then, they both went to the fire to check the supper. The boy saw them prepare the plates, and then his father beckoned him and finally, raising his voice, said, "Supper..."

The boy turned away and stared out at the lake, the waves rougher now, drumming the shoreline. The water encircled his feet, then receded, leaving small pools of scum and strands of seaweed around them.

"Stephen," he heard his father yelling to him again, "get over here right now."

He half turned toward the far end of the beach and saw Eva touch his father's shoulder and whisper to him. Then, she was walking toward him with a bowl and spoon in her hand.

He watched her approach. She was looking at him intently, wrapped in her terrycloth robe, leaving wet imprints in the sand that were erased by the lap of the tide. Finally, she was standing before him, offering the steaming bowl of stew, smiling.

"I brought you some supper, Stephen. I know you must be so hungry. Here, eat it," she spoke gently.

He stared at her, then shook his head and turned away angrily. But she sat down next to him on the log and placed an arm around his shoulder. He shuddered and shook off her hand and made as if to move away.

"Oh come on, Stephen. Be a dear. Eat. Besides, how can you be angry at me? Don't you love me anymore?" She continued: "Look, I've forgotten what happened out there and I've spoken to your father so he won't be angry with you anymore. Come on now, let's put it all behind us."

He turned to her, furious, and tried to speak, but she drew him to her and he felt the warmth of her nakedness under the half-opened robe and saw the outline of a breast before she arranged herself, smiling secretly. Confused and embarrassed, he looked down at the bowl of stew resting on the log beside Eva. She caught his gaze and picked up the bowl and held it out to him.

"Eat."

Then, she reached in with her fingers and extracted a large morsel of the succulent meat and bit off half of it offering the other half to him, all the while smiling, her eyes never leaving his face. He took the meat from her finger into his mouth while she laughed, gaily at first, then more harshly, finally jeering at him.

"You silly, stupid boy. Eat now. It's all over."

And he did take the bowl from her and watched her walk back to the fire, her back straight, never once looking back at him.

Finally, he stared down at the bowl and the untouched food and spat the half-chewed morsel from his mouth as he felt the tightness in his chest burst open like a great bubble until the tears began to roll down his cheeks to land in the water gathering around his feet and disappear back into the inexorable pull of the tide.

Revolver

Anushree Varma

Revolver

I'm lying here, two fingers to my temple, pulling the trigger.

It's cold, the hard stone floor. Worse, because I am naked. When they found me tearing my dress off myself, tying the strips of it into a noose, they started ripping the rest off. The woman held me down, the man pulled my dress away. When I screamed, they pulled harder. No blue god came, with silk flowing from his hand to save me from the humiliation of being stripped naked. No. So I had to fight them off myself, and I did, until I couldn't anymore. But then the man made the mistake of hushing me, of stroking my thighs. I don't want to ever be touched like that — now that I know what comes of it. I felt my body flailing, thrashing against his touch.

There are prisons you put yourself in, prisons others put you in. I am in both.

They'll tell you they brought me down here in handcuffs, but that's not true. No, it was me. I called and I called and finally the earth opened up, the sidewalk beneath my feet grew muddy, soft. I started slipping, pulled down into the black, gaping mouth of this monster.

In this darkness, two interrogators stood before me. A black-haired man, dressed in blue, with vivid blue eyes. A tall woman with a coarse mane. "What's your name?" the man asked. When I said nothing, the lion woman growled at me. They were angry because they couldn't figure out who I was. From my accent, they knew I was a foreigner, a visitor, but from where? They took my fingerprints, and I looked at the smudges, falling lost into the whorls. "Where did you get that gun?" asked the woman. The silver hand dangling from her keychain caught my eye. "From the Hand of Fatima," I answered "Slut!" she snapped, smacking it across my face. "Don't you know what trouble you're in?" But this stone precinct of hers doesn't fool me. This old police station, with its pillars and carved lotuses, made to look like a temple, to terrify me that even the gods or Fatima's living hand, covered with henna and heavy silver rings didn't reach out for me either.

"Take her down," said the woman, "let her rot alone." The blue man pulled me away, past a family waiting on a bench, a black family. The unhappy mother sat with her huge legs spread wide, head slumped back, eye swollen shut like a purple clam. Her husband had their pretty little daughter squirming in his lap, her finger in her mouth. He looked down at her, in horror and pity, as if only now realizing that such innocence always invites what destroys it. His wife suddenly came to life, howling, "Where is my son? Give me his body!" I turned, to go to her, but the blue man dragged me away.

"Don't," the lion woman cried out, as I left, "don't think that I'll help you! I'm not your sister! I despise your kind, ruining things for the rest of us…" She's not the only one who despises me.

Lying on this cold floor, other figures come, accusing. Noémi stands, as she did that night, cursing me with her eyes. At Le Chat Qui Fume, the little nightclub in Montmartre where we went dancing. In alcoves, customers were lying against pillows, smoking huqqas. They were playing music mixed with old Arabic songs of the 40s. Through the smoke and the whirling dancers, Karim — her Karim — came to me, and I didn't turn away. Noémi — her hurt, confused face, a ribbon twisting on her brown shoulder, confetti falling, the pearls drooping from her ears, watching us. Was I cruel to her? Yes, I was — and so was he, but love is cruel, isn't it, when it cuts another out? Or at least mine was.

I felt the heavy curse of that guilt upon me. For that is what guilt is, a curse upon one's self. Witch doctors know this by instinct, and others, who whip up our guilt, knowing it will be our downfall.

But my happiness was flowering. I didn't question. I was a little drunk, reckless. I twined my arm around Karim's neck and let him turn me, turn me away. His hand on the small of my back, firm. When a man takes you into his arms to dance, his hand there tells you all you need to know about him. The serpent coiling in my tailbone was rising up, up.

Doors clang. "And so," I hear another officer whispering to the blue one, "how is our little terrorist?" This guard is blonde, proud of the golden waves on his head, preening. When he looks at me, he sees only my nudity. It's a kind of rape — the way he looks. The worst kind of rape — loveless, violent. And I realize I have never been naked before a man like this unless he was my lover — or, it was summer, and we were in the privacy of the long dark sea. The blue guard never looks at me, my body. When I look at him, his shocked blue eyes turn away but his knuckles whiten.

"How long can we leave her like that?" he asks. "The longer the better, don't you think?" laughs the blonde. "They won't even let me give her a blanket." "No! of course not," protests the other, "you can't always keep an eye on her, and you saw what she was doing with her dress — the last thing we need is a woman swinging in a cell. The newspapers would murder us again." The blue guard flinches at this. "We should send her to the women's ward then, or the hospital," he says. "Blame the bitch upstairs," the blonde replies, "she wants to hold onto her, to get her to talk. She thinks the little slut knows something about the guns pouring in from Africa..."

I fall asleep. I dream of shifting sands, of a camel's head loping against the sky.

"Those guns, you know, are pointing at us," says the blonde, stroking the one in his holster. I wake to the men still talking. "They've got guns and most of us, like fools, in shields and helmets, with our sticks. Last night, one bastard was firing off two shots at a time, reloading in a stairwell, coming back out. Bang, bang! firing again! But you can't lose your nerve. I took him in, and another guy, looting a jeweler's." He stops, and sighs, "It's hell — be happy you're not out there anymore, with me."

But he says it with a slight taunting edge to his voice, as if to tell the other man just the opposite, that he is nothing without his gun, his power, his nerve. The blue guard, who wears no gun, bristles. "OK, Yves," he says, "so long." When he calls him Yves, a long branch of lightning pierces me. I know then that he, the blonde guard, Yves, is the one who ruined me, who is to blame for my misery. He is why I am here. I look up to see his face leering at me from behind the bars, like a white baboon.

Holding my knees to myself, my fingers run over my skin, feeling the mole beneath my breast, the curves and folds of me, the down on my body. I fall asleep, mumbling of Zulu warriors, with bead and feather necklaces, of wild things who die overnight in prison. Their bodies trapped, their spirits just go…

After that night of dancing, Karim and I went home together. We walked down the slopes of Montmartre where once were lush purple vineyards and windmills, now narrow cobbled streets. African men in pillbox hats and bright djelabas selling beads of amber and ebony, called out to us as we went by. We might have walked all night, or stayed listening to the Senegalese girls singing so passionately, round a bin of fire, warming their hands.

But without saying a word, we headed to my narrow room in the Marais. Past the crumbling synagogue in its gold dome, its high stone walls hairy with weeds. Gone were the evening scholars, with their Talmud and Torah, gone were the bakers and watchmakers. The river was spotted with stars, the city was ablaze. The bridges arched their backs like angry cats. A whore laughed at both customer and pimp, arguing her price. Hotels, brasseries, bistros. And the men, the dark men in the off hours sitting among the crates at the backdoors, in white aprons, smoking, brooding, discontent. We arrived. A mysterious blue moon shone down through my window. I stared at it with my back turned to Karim, as he unbuttoned me. The soft waving hair on my neck, all over my body, sprang up. My dress crumpled noisily around my waist as his hands went to my hips, pulling me onto himself.

"Your hair," he moaned, "smells of jasmine."
Jasmine, oh voluptuous white buds, spilling perfume. Every night at dusk, a donkey sniffs them outside Karim's grandmother's house, far away in the countryside of his native Algeria. "You look like you're from there," he said. "But I'm not," I said, moodily. "What are you afraid of?" he laughed, winding the bed sheet around me like a burqa, like the scarves of a Touareg, so that only my eyes showed. "Don't," I said, pulling away. He looked at me, thoughtfully. "I suppose in your country, my people and yours are killing each other," he said.

Ours was the cosmic attraction of enemies, inevitable as that of brother and sister separated in infancy, to find themselves years later, unknowingly, under the wedding canopy.

My father was cut out of his mother's womb by a soldier's sword, saved, while she died, her throat slit by Moslem knives on a train out of Lahore, in 1947. Arriving at the station, the silent carriage was full of corpses lying about as if asleep, their necks cut by long red smiles. Out of this violent blood, my father was born. And it hadn't stopped. Only yesterday, the newspaper had mentioned the lynching of a Hindu girl and a Moslem boy they ran away to get married and returned, a year later, to find their whole village still furious.

"That might have been us," I said to Karim who put his fingers on my lips. But no — this world saw us as one, not different from each other. "Arabe," spat a woman at us, hurrying by on the street. "Go back where you come from," she snarled. "Go to hell where you come from," shouted Karim, livid. I could be from many places but his ancestry was unmistakable. His face, its long sharp black brows, was of the desert. Its only chink was the eye that twitched when he was tired or upset, or sad.

"What does she mean to where we come from?" I asked, trying to humor him back. "To the womb? Or to the arms of some black Eve? Or to a past life, or —" "Why don't you ask her," snapped Karim. "Bitch!" he cried, turning back to where the woman was disappearing. I pulled him on, past the kiosks of roses and tiger lilies.

I wake again, coughing. Yves, the blonde guard, is squatting, blowing smoke through the bars. "Want one?" he smirks, proffering the torn packet. "A smoke," I reply, "how perfect. My last before the firing squad?" He slowly exhales, burning his awful eyes into me. "Ah," he smiles, "so you do talk." I want a cigarette so badly but I turn away. For once, I don't give into my blood's cravings.

With Karim, I gave in completely. "For you," I said to him, giving him a hand mirror wrapped in tissue. He tore it off, smiling uncertainly. "You think I'm vain," he remarked. "The gift," I said, kneeling before him, "is what I want you to see in it." I took the hand that held the mirror, bringing it down beside my face so that he could watch what I was doing to him. Me, my twin, my triplet. And though I knelt, I felt my own power.

Later, lying in bed, I admitted I didn't know what I looked like there, between my legs. Someone playing a violin in another apartment, broke off, the twang hanging in the air. "There?" he asked, surprised. I nodded. "You don't know?" I shook my head, suddenly embarrassed, like having confessed I couldn't write my name or say my aleph bey. He sat up abruptly, pulling me onto his lap, opening up my thighs, showing me myself. I put my arms around his neck and hid my face, scared to look. I was shaking, seasick. I don't know why it terrified me so to see myself, the source of me. "Look," he said softly. A dark-tipped, almost black flower, primitive, ancient, eternal. I felt as when, as a child, I held in my palms a throbbing little bird — it frightened me, how alive it was, how near death, how naked, hungry.

That night we ate at Le P'tit Chaoui, in the onzième. Its walls hung with Berber rugs, Bedouin paraphernalia, darboukas and tambourines. The faces of the few other patrons, distorted in the chrome of the coffee machine, burst out laughing. I felt we were nomads passing through, like a thought the world has, then soon forgets. The waitress brought us a tajin of steaming vegetables and meat, a plate of couscous. We lingered over cheap sour wine, laughing when a little of it spilled on my green dress...

On the way home, Karim stopped at a tabagie to buy cigarettes. Waiting for his change, he leaned towards me, kissing my mouth, above the bright flowers in buckets. I looked over his shoulder at the hanging packets of tobacco covered with pictures of Zouave soldiers, dressed in crimson fez and exotic blue braided coats.

"Look," I said. A black sun graced the front page of Le Figaro, "a total eclipse in Africa." Karim tore open his pack of cigarettes, drew one out and lit it. "I saw an eclipse once," he said, "when I was very young. My father and I were walking together in the woods. The sky grew dark, stars coming out though it was noon, clouds of birds flying screaming into the trees, shadows flowing like ribbons. When the sun went black, my father covered my eyes. I was very afraid but I held onto his hand and that made me brave. Then he said now you will see that all of this will quickly go away. And it did. I thought my father knew everything." "And did he?" I smiled. "No," said Karim, bleakly.

The dirty streets of Oberkampf were rolling in litter but the old buildings around us looked on, secretive. One was all of white bones, gutted. It had burnt down, the fire smoking out a swarm of hidden Somalian children and their mothers — second, third, and fourth wives — squatting there. "Arson," said Karim. A radio on a sill blared live from the Opéra, another hiphop. A crowd of pretty girls in cowl necks swung by, on the arms of their boys. A man pulled on by his big black poodle. Young turks on mopeds, speeding off.

Then the street was ours alone.

From an alley, a cat with spirals on its coat came out to brush softly against our legs. I stopped, bending down to stroke it. We heard the shot then. The cat scampered off. Turning the corner, a boy came running towards us, racing, his bones bursting through his skin. His black face was terrified, tearstained. Crashing into us, he stopped, a revolver dangling from his hand. He opened his mouth, to say something. But just then a siren began keening. Panicking, he threw the revolver down at our feet where it hit the stones spinning. The boy tried to fling himself over a wall but he was too late. The cops arrived, sirens flashing. The boy screamed, "No! Don't shoot! I'll give you the money!" As he reached into his pocket, a shot rang out. And then another, and another. Hidden in the shadows, nobody saw Karim and me. I tried to run to the boy but Karim held me back. "No," he cried, his face aghast, "they'll shoot you too!" "He's dead," someone said.

Not a mirage, I saw the ghost of the dead boy kneeling on the gleaming pool of his own blood, looking down at his face.

Karim pulled me away, into a taxi. Two jackal-faced women at my front door broke off talking when they saw us. As soon as we were upstairs, Karim pulled out the revolver from his pocket, staring down at it. I hadn't seen him pick it up. "My god!" I cried, scared. I took it, shoved it into the red-lined drawer of my dresser, slamming it shut, hoping it would disappear. Trembling, we fell into bed, too sick to say anything.

But soon Karim woke out of a nightmare into my arms, fighting me off, weeping hot angry tears. "Why didn't I go?" he cried out. "Why didn't I go?" His father, he told me then, had been a journalist in Algiers. There were threats but he refused to recant, refused to stop writing. One afternoon, the police pulled him out of his car in front of their home and shot him. Karim, only a boy, had seen it all from the terrace above, one of his homing pigeons landing on his fist.

I slept fitfully that night, my body anointed with that rarest of waters, the tears of a man.

It was different from then on, for us. At night we lay awake, apart, without even sleep to hold us together. We listened to the angry roar rising in the streets. It was all over the newspapers, how an unarmed Tunisian boy, having robbed a tabagie, was shot dead in the street. The torches of fires lit in vigil soon began burning down the city, setting ablaze its cars, shops, schools and its library.

Now Karim wanted to join in. "Don't," he said, when I started to cry. I knew then, I already knew what was to come. His face was tortured. "Don't ask me to be less than I want to be." "It's crazy," I cried. "Is it?" he retorted. "All I know is that not doing what I have to do makes me crazy." He, who had held me back that night, now hated me for holding him back.

That night, while he was sleeping, I woke up and went to my dressing table. I took the revolver out, in a trance. I began twirling it on my finger, playing with it. Bang! I whispered to myself in the mirror, pointing the gun at my reflection. Who was I? I didn't know, I never had. Bang, bang. I saw Karim then, lifting up on one elbow in the bed behind, dazed. My hand seemed to suddenly have a life of its own, the revolver went off. The looking glass shivered and shattered, our faces splintering. "My god!" he cried, leaping up, wrenching the revolver away. He put it back in the drawer, slamming it shut. I wept while he held me all night, his arms twined hard around me. But between us, the embryo of something was slipping away.

The next evening I said nothing when he left. How long can you keep anybody from their fate? It was the worst night of rioting yet. Rocks, molotovs, firebombs, children with guns. The holy and unholy warriors, dancing in orange flames and billowing smoke. By morning, Karim was dead. An officer by the name of Yves L — shot him in the chest.

I'm screaming now, so loudly, it doesn't seem to be my voice.

The blue officer throws open the rattling bars, kneels down beside me. "Karim," I call out. His face is shocked as looks down. "Oh my god," he groans. "Don't, don't punish yourself like this — please don't." "You don't know," I say, "you don't know." "I know what it is to give up hope," he answers, "I know what it is to fear, to fear so much you do crazy things. I —" I start crying then). His arms go around me, as he rocks me back and forth, singing to me. His voice husky, fevered, desperate. And then it is the rhythms, his and mine, the rhythms of rocking, of heart, and breath. That's all we are, these rhythms, these beats. And maybe that is what will become of me when I die. My blood, my bones, my flesh, all of me, I will be taken back into the music.

After Karim's death, I didn't leave the house for days. And when I did, the world was unfamiliar, unwanted. Its towers fingers pointing nowhere. The newspapers spat at me. The police were closing ranks — the officer who killed Karim was not going to be punished. It was the circumstances, they said, the terrible times. The only thing I wanted to do was blot myself out so I bought whiskey to drown myself in, my pain. But spirits don't drown the angry spirits within us, they only join forces together. I made up my mind to do something.

I called Horace, the pusher at the Sphinxe, a bar in Montparnasse that I used to go to. His roots went deep into the underground, or so he bragged. "Enfin cherie," he said through the thrum of the music, "you've remembered me." "I want a favour," I said, as silkily as I could. "Ah," he drawled, "I've got some pretty little pills just for you." "Not that," I said, surprising him with my request. Half an hour later he phoned back. "Yves L is working at such and such precinct, and yes, he is on duty tonight. But why do you want to know?" I said nothing. "When do I see you?" he sighed. "I'll haunt you," I said, hanging up.

I put on my scarlet dress. I opened the red-lined drawer, and pulled out the revolver. I had no pockets in my dress, so I tucked it into my garter. Karim would have liked this film noir touch, I thought, posing in the mirror as if he were beyond it. I had a drink. Not that I needed courage when I had rage. I headed out.

I don't know when the desire for revenge took root in me, but by the time I caught a whiff of it, it was in full bloom. Outside, I felt wildly happy, free, as if my soul were lifting its wings. I threw back my head, singing. Startled faces turned. Others, in broad rimmed black hats and lush fur robes, hurried away. I sang and sang — perverse maybe, but I wanted to leave the world singing. I was overflowing with joy, the terror at what I was going to do had melted away. A crowd of kids followed me. I wanted to say goodbye then, to the world that I had desired, but that had disappointed me. Like a lover wised-up at last, I knew it was time to go. So I climbed the yew tree, the yew tree with the moon in its fingers. I looked out to the city.

And then suddenly, I didn't care anymore.

I was tired, so tired. And it wasn't worth it, suffering like this. For what? The sadness settled into me like a flock of black birds. Sitting in the crotch of the yew, I took out my revolver. Bang, bang, bang. People scattered, screaming, as I picked off the stars. When the sirens rose, I put the revolver to my temple, and fired. But nothing, no bullet. I kept pulling the trigger as they pulled me down, out of the tree.

Now here I am, lying on the floor, dying of the cold. A thin man with a big black falcon head, in blue jeans, comes to me. The bird god, wanting to weigh my soul against a feather. What can I say to one I can't lie to? No, I haven't caused pain. No, I haven't eaten my heart out. No I haven't, I haven't…

I wake to find the blonde watching me, my fingers at my temple. "This what you want?" he asks, pulling out his revolver, twirling it. Only it's not his. This one is different. It's mine. "I brought it for you," he whispers, cocking it, "and it's loaded." He moves closer. "Just like me." He fumbles with his keys, unlocking the door. He falls into the cell. He falls on my nakedness, on me. "No," I cry, "no!" He puts the gun to me and I feel my body, through the terror, flailing. "Don't," he pants, "don't pretend you don't want it, lying there like that, driving me crazy." The more I fight, the wilder he gets, the more he seems to enjoy it. And there's so little to do, I'm already naked.

Then he screams.

I look up to see another face, one with wild angry blue eyes,

Touareg blue, falling towards us. "What the fuck?" cries the blonde, caught in the tangle of his trousers. The blue guard pulls him off me. The revolver flies. While the two men thrash, I grab the gun, run out of the cell, slam the door shut and turn the key. The men are still pounding each other. "Hey!" I call. They ignore me. "Hey, hey, hey," I scream. They look up at me, their faces freezing. "Oh no," says the blonde, seeing the keys in my hand. I point the gun at him as he shakes his head. "No," he stutters, "don't, please."

"Yves L—," I say, as I cock the trigger. His mouth drops. "L—?" he gasps, "but I'm not L—." He points to the other guard. "He is!" The man on the floor beside him, the other Yves, mine, looks up at me with the bluest eyes. For once, our eyes meet, and hold. "Now you know," he says, "at last." Slowly he rises, spreading out his palms. "Shoot me," he whispers, "go ahead, please."

Bang, I whisper. Bang, bang, bang.

No one falls. No blood anywhere but where it should be, flowing within. "Take off your clothes," I say. They look at each other. I shake my gun at them. "Hurry!" I cry, and they do. Now they are both naked, raw, their bodies red and limp. Never have I seen naked men look so miserable. The black-haired one stands quietly, watching me. But the blonde shakes the bars, yelling, "Whore! You'll never make it out of here!" I'm in blue when I leave.

Nobody, not even the lion woman sees me, slipping through corridors, out and away.

Dawn is breaking, birds shrieking. I go to the Seine.

In the filthy water, the city is drowning, quivering, alive.

Off the bridge, I drop the revolver, but keep a bullet, a tear, my dark souvenir.

Rendez-vous

Greta Hofmann Nemiroff

Rendez-vous

Many years before this time, when she first became a mother, Ella would find herself rendering into precise line drawings the intermittent appearances of the Angel of Death. She'd picture the Angel winding her skinny arms alarmingly around the plump perfection of Ruthie, her baby daughter, or in the act of violently snatching the child from her cradle. People admired these drawings, which were large and full of movement, but no one ever spoke directly to her about her subject matter.

In time, while Ruthie grew and flourished, Ella moved on to other subjects, until finally she stopped drawing altogether and become a professor of art history. Ruthie now is an adult, living with her children on the other side of Canada, and Ella has not thought about the Angel of Death until recently. Now, however, as she is sitting on the cold marble stairs facing her locked apartment door, the Angel of Death flits through her thoughts while she tries to concentrate on reciting a mantra she has invented (or perhaps plagiarized, she can't remember): "Breathe in, breathe out, breathe in, breathe out…" and again…and again.

She is surrounded by her luggage plus a duty-free bag containing not-so-bargain bottles of Scotch and Opium, a perfume she loves. Despite her calming words to herself, she cannot fully repress the question that haunts her: where could she have lost the keys? In Khaled's apartment in Beirut? In the hotel in Damascus? In the desert near Palmyra when she paid the Bedouin carpet salesman? When she bought those sweets in the airport in Amman? Surely she would have heard the keys drop. She has left an emergency telephone message for Julio, the concierge, and she is waiting for him to arrive with his keys.

Ella gets up and presses her ear against the rough layered varnish of the apartment door. There is no sound, no movement. Usually Molly, her elderly cat, is right by the door as soon as she hears Ella enter the building. Surely there can be no cause for alarm. Annamaria, Julio's teenaged daughter, has been taking care of her, and Ella has paid her well in advance.

Ella doesn't like to think about a life without Molly. She often jokes with her friends when they broach the question of a widowhood romance to her: "Are you kidding? I just got my life back. I'm not a nursemaid any more. I'm retired and I've got my health. Molly and I will march into old age together...like two sisters!" She realizes that some people have found this parody of spinsterhood surprising and even annoying after her long marriage, but she feels she's earned the right to assume any identity she cares to create. Phil's end had been brutal; she'd been relieved when the cancer had finally killed him. It isn't that she hasn't mourned him. She's gone through it all...the terrible knowledge that she'd never see or touch him again, the shock of waking up to an empty bed, having to plan her weekends well in advance if she didn't want to be alone, not having anyone with whom to share her daily trivia. She's eventually come to enjoy her newly acquired habit of falling asleep sharing her bed with Molly, surrounded by books and a pretty lacquered tray with her dental floss, comb, sleeping pills, nail polish, pens and paper, and a cup of tea where Phil's head used to be.

She sits back on the stairs and wraps her coat and shawl tightly against the April cold seeping into the building. There must be some reason for Molly's silence. Cats do like sleeping during the day and it's only mid afternoon here in Montreal. She feels as if it were midnight and longs for a hot bath and the comfort of her duvet, her tray, and Molly purring at her side.

The last minutes in Beirut with Khaled were difficult and stiff. When he wished her a safe journey, she couldn't resist replying: "Thanks, I need a bit of luck. It seems that I've been only one step ahead of the Angel of Death since I left Montreal."

Khaled had frowned a bit and she'd caught the flicker of irritation in his eyes, but he'd been mild. "Don't be superstitious. It's not like you," he'd said.

By the forced evenness of his tone, she had comprehended immediately that what he wanted was that their last conversation be light, free of "heavy emotion," mutual recrimination or disappoint-ment. As he'd said several times, it was nobody's fault things hadn't exactly clicked between them. "As a scientist, "he'd smiled remotely in that café they'd enjoyed on the Corniche, "I know our lives are composed of innumerable instances of trial and error." By that time they had already stopped including the future in their conversations.

But it all started so hopefully, she'd wanted to say, though she'd remained silent. Or as hopefully as anything could between two seasoned and retired academics. Their mutual friend, Saadia, had brought them together. "I've got a soul mate for you, Ella," she'd said, "the husband of a distant cousin in Beirut. He's been a widower for some years. He's a retired engineering professor and his kids live in the US. He comes over at least once a year. I think you'd like each other so I'm going to give him your email address, OK?"

And why not? It wasn't as if she were aching for romance, but it would be nice, she'd thought as many women in her situation think, to have a companion, someone with whom to share what she thought of as her "end years," even if mainly through the Internet. There was also the appealing "otherness" of him, so different from her roots in western Ontario. It surprised her how addictive their email relationship quickly became. They had life times to recreate, shape and present to one another through this medium. From prudent weekly exchanges, they'd accelerated to daily messages and then to contacting one another several times a day. At the beginning they had exchanged rather formal information on the better moments of their modestly successful careers. Then they'd written carefully about their respective children and grandchildren. They had brushed very lightly on their deceased spouses. But soon they were discussing their tastes: he loved various Middle Eastern singers she'd never heard whose songs he sent over the Internet. She loved Beethoven and jazz, but since she'd never learned the technology of sending the music directly to him, she'd gone the long way, sending him CDs. They both loved Shakespeare, and she learned to appreciate Rumi on his recommendation. They would write amusing little vignettes of their every day life to one another. They even had touched tactfully on their religious differences, only to affirm that they were both only nominally, sentimentally perhaps, attached: he to the Islam practiced within his family and she to vague memories of the kindly United Church of her childhood. Flattering photos were emailed. She presented herself in her favourite blue blouse, her auburn hair refreshed by the hairdresser. He'd concealed his bald spot and focused on the strong features and warmth of his smile. After some months it was only logical that they meet: he invited her to visit him in Beirut.

Breathing deeply had almost failed her on the plane during the first leg of the journey and at Heathrow. Someone had died on the way to London; a woman with cancer, it was gossiped through the aisles, who had come to Montreal to say goodbye to her parents. She had not survived the trip home to London. This mischance had been treated skillfully by the crew. The woman's husband had stood by, ashen faced, while his wife was covered and tucked away in her seat. The death cast its pall, nonetheless, although Ella could not remember having seen the woman alive. In great agitation, she'd walked up and down the neon-laden airport hallways, thinking of booking an immediate ticket back to Montreal. In a world where someone could be snatched away like that, how could she put her faith in so tenuous a relationship, she'd wondered. There was a long wait between planes and her ruminations exhausted her. Finally she reasoned that she could leave Beirut whenever she wanted; she was curious about this man, Khaled.

Suspended in time on the staircase, Ella realizes that she isn't surprised that things didn't work out that well with Khaled. This was not due to their different cultures or even their very reserved and stiff sexual encounters. There were bodily shames between them: the depredations of gravity on their bodies made nudity reluctant and the paucity of exposed skin a constant reproach. They had enjoyed one another's company, but not wholeheartedly. There was always a tentative carefulness underlying their times together. It just didn't seem worth while to work toward any kind of future together. Ella could not overcome her feeling that the Angel of Death was accompanying her on this voyage; the occasional brush of the Angel's leathery wing was, at the very least, unsettling. She'd wanted to sweep up to the Angel and shake her until her bones rattled, shouting "Not now, later! Come-Back-Later!" very loudly and slowly as if talking to a deaf foreigner.

One day they went to Khaled's family village in the south of Lebanon for the funeral of a cousin, a man who had been a chauffeur to people high in government. His connections had done much for the village. She had no idea how Khaled had explained her presence to the widow, a hunched silent figure dwarfed by a huge velour arm chair and guarded by the looming protection of four sons, all of them ugly. Ella had been relegated to the women's balcony on one side of the building. She could talk to no one although the women, chatting energetically among themselves, had all nodded at her in a seemingly friendly manner. Caterers went back and forth delivering elaborate plates of food. Her view of the driveway recorded the continual arrival of groups of mourners, including a phalanx of Druze men in black high collared suits and conical white hats.

The corpse had not been buried as fast as it should have been; it had lain in a deep freeze until the four sons could be gathered from their corners of America. It was a warm day for April. Suddenly it was noticed that a puddle was forming under the table on which the shrouded body was lying. Efficiently and somewhat roughly, the body was rushed to a truck; all the men accompanied it to its burial, but women were not to be included in that ritual.

Ella had tried to distance herself by adopting an anthropological perspective towards the event, but the sight of the body being borne away, its damp shroud revealing an unmistakable shape, stayed with her for the rest of her time in Lebanon. She suspected that the Angel of Death was crouched in the shrubbery by the women's veranda, watching, watching.

Ella and Khaled had learned, separately and together, that they were better off traveling than staying in Khaled's apartment in Beirut. Although it was an attractive modern apartment with a view of the Mediterranean and near the American University, neither of them felt comfortable with the inevitable domesticity of this arrangement. Despite the best of intentions they had lapsed into stereotypical roles: he watched the news and sports on TV while she prepared dinner and cleaned up. Through traveling, they were able to present a more authentic version of themselves as the gregarious shipboard like companions they were. In that way they could quite contentedly occupy the stern twin-bedded room at the Queen Zenobia Palace Hotel in Palmyra. There, with other tourists, they could enjoy a long drink on the terrace watching the spectacular desert sun set on ancient avenues of excavated Nabatean ruins. They demanded so little of one another, while presenting to the world a seemly diorama of the happily retired couple, well heeled, reasonably attractive, and generally benign. No questions were ever asked about their relationship, nor did she ask if Palmyra was really called Tadmor, the site of one of Syria's most wretched and dangerous prisons. They'd stood on the walls of a citadel high up on a mountain and enjoyed the view of the desert and distant salt marshes.

There was something liberating about traveling in the desert, bargaining in Khaled's presence for Bedouin rugs for her country house in the Laurentians. She'd also reveled in her indifference to Khaled's purchases for himself, ongoing evidence of his other, his "real" life. Their travels held them suspended in time and sentiment through the beauties of Syria. They joked companionably over the omnipresent gigantic portraits on the sides of buildings of the unprepossessing presidential incumbent and his equally homely late father. Traveling to good places, having excellent and interesting meals, and enjoying the pleasant appointments of medium priced hotels, Ella was gratefully free of intimations of mortality. In her thoughts she would crow that living well was truly the best way to vanquish reminders of mortality.

The Angel of Death did not put in a full appearance until they went to Amman to visit Khaled's sister Noor and her husband Hassan, an aging physician. They had recently moved into an apartment in an expensive enclave of dazzlingly white marble square buildings. Their home was well appointed and luxuriously furnished. The building was serviced by a young janitor, Ali, who was generously tipped for many extra services rendered to Hassan and other occupants.

On their last day, they came upon Ali sitting on the stairs in front of the building, crying wildly and conspicuously. His howls echoed off the white buildings. Hassan was standing beside him, trying to comfort him. "He has received a call from Aleppo," Hassan confided to them in his accented but excellent English. "His mother has died and they want him to return immediately." Ali's eyes were wild and red; from time to time he would subside into long shuddering sighs that brought into relief his ribcage, long dirty nails clutching the top of his head. A group of tenants formed around him; they kept passing money to him as he continued weeping while carefully examining and then folding each bill into his pocket. When Hassan tried to edge him back into the building, however, Ali would resist, his cries would become louder, his mouth wide open, revealing the decay and dark spaces wrought by a life of poverty.

It was then that Fatima, Ali's somewhat older wife, appeared from the basement. She was carrying a large basket of newly ironed and folded laundry to deliver to one of the tenants. She was a tall stocky woman with her hair pulled off her face in a severe bun. When she appeared, Ali immediately stopped howling. "It's nothing," she calmly assured the crowd, "it's nothing. I don't believe his mother is dead. They always do this when they want money. He's a good son and gives it to them. Why do they lie to him? He will send money anyway. They want him to come to them so they can squeeze even more money out of him." She tapped him heavily on the shoulder. "Get up and come in," she said. "It is time to eat. First take this laundry up to the third floor and hurry. Your meal is ready." She turned her back on them all and made her way unflinchingly through the crowd. Without a further sound, Ali picked up the basket and entered the building. The tenants shook their heads at one another. No one said anything; they appeared somewhat ashamed for having been duped.

Ella stayed behind, paralyzed with recognition. She could see that the young man was somewhat histrionic, but the Angel of Death had revealed herself and frightened him. Ali had met with mortality and made excellent use of this event by eliciting and accepting both sympathy and monetary compensation. She wondered if she could be so crass with her secret visions; she had only been able to draw them. She had never put them into words…even as untruths.

The remembered feeling of standing frozen in thought in front of a luxury dwelling so far from home has brought her back to her own modest staircase. She can hear the telephone ringing behind the locked door. Who could it be she wonders. It could be Ruthie, anxious to hear her news. How had it worked out with that man? Why had she stopped answering Ruthie's emails after the second week? Ella imagines the ambivalence Ruthie must feel, wanting her to enjoy life, but on the other hand not accepting another "father." Whoever it may be, Ella reminds herself, there is voice mail. It is the cat that captures her thoughts now. She imagines herself roaming the apartment looking for Molly, making her favourite calling sounds into the silence. She quickly confects the fatalistic rationalization that after all Molly is fifteen years old and has diabetes, requiring two injections of insulin a day. Even with good care, the veterinarian has assured her, the cat's health is poor. She imagines finding the cat on the floor in a corner of the guest room, lying on her back with stiffened legs straight in the air, her striped coat already dull and shedding. She can see the glassiness of the animal's final stare at the world. How will she dispose of Molly, she wonders in a panic at the same time as she tells herself to drop the subject. What good can come from this panic? It will not be the first time the Angel of Death has outwitted her.

She doesn't know why she confided her vision to Khaled when they returned to Beirut. Perhaps it was because he raised the subject on their last evening. They had finished an excellent candle-lit dinner in one of the better cafés spread along the Corniche. The view was splendid, even in the dark with the play of lights around them and a white ruffle of surf gently brushing the shore. Above them, the lights of Beirut glimmered half way up the distant mountains. Khaled had been amused by the scene with Ali and by Ella's initially being so moved by the young man's histrionics.

"You mean you didn't believe him from the beginning?" she'd asked.

"Not fully," he'd answered. "Why would he scream and cry in front of the building except to extort money? He's a poor young man who depends on tips. Perhaps they were not up to par this month." Khaled laughed lightly, without malice or judgment." That's the way things are here. People must find their way. You do not really understand poor countries. Of course in America you don't have servants the way we do. We take it for granted that they will try to get what they can from us."

Ella was stung by this "third world" accusation of the perverse privilege of not being cheated in one's house because one could not afford servants. "I have my own reasons for being moved by him." She explained her experiences with the Angel of Death, savouring the act of narration. "Sometimes I feel the Angel flying too close," she'd mentioned. "I can hear the whir of feathers and feel the leatheriness of her wings as she brushes past me."

Khaled had looked somewhat annoyed by her revelations, but he had been careful to smile indulgently. "You people in the arts love metaphors, don't you? Of course we all know we are going to die, but one doesn't have to dwell upon these things. There's so much else to life." He'd flung out his arm in embrace of the scene. "The better things in life are certainly a compensation for its brevity. No one wants to die, but it strikes me as being impractical to waste one's time dwelling on it when there is so much to enjoy, no?"

Ella would have loved to agree with him, because in truth she had enjoyed the varied landscapes through which Khaled had conducted her. However, she had felt an obligation to clarify her experience. "It's not a metaphor," she'd stubbornly maintained, "it's a fact of my life."

By Khaled's shrug, she'd understood that she had been dismissed. In a world full of abandoned women of a certain age, who would want to take on someone with her vision? True, she knew she could play the competent rational professor, but the intermittent appearances of the Angel of Death formed the very underpinning of her consciousness. The evening had disintegrated into her final packing and an unsaid but mutual pact of politesse from which they hadn't deviated. Wordlessly negotiated pleasantness prevailed between them until she walked through the metal detector at the airport. On the way home, she decided that if there were ever to be another stab at companionship in her life, she'd keep the presence of the Angel of Death to herself. Perhaps, she reflected, older men did not like to be reminded of their mortality; they would not recognize the angel if they saw her.

She can hear Julio opening the inside door at the bottom of the stairs; Annamaria is with him. They are jovial with welcome as they unlock her apartment; Julio carries her suitcases and thanks her profusely for the bottle of Scotch.

"Have you seen the cat, today? "she anxiously asks Anamaria.

"Yes, I gave her a shot and fed her this morning," Anamaria says. "She likes to hide. I'll find her for you."

Ella hurries directly to the guest room and, as she has imagined, the cat is there, but very much alive and asleep on the frilled and flowered pillows. She indifferently accepts Ella's caresses and quickly escapes, jumping stiffly off the bed.

"She's alive!" Ella exclaims then stops, seeing the look of hurt on Anamaria's conscientious young face.

"I came to look after her twice a day like I promised, missus." Anamaria's voice raises in piqued defiance.

"Oh, Anamaria, I know you did your best. But sometimes the Angel of Death appears anyway," Ella speaks soothingly. "She is an old cat."

Julio seems to sense incipient discord. "It's time for supper, " he says to Anamaria. "Thank you, missus, for the Scotch. Anamaria's a good girl, you know. Any time you want help..." and they are gone.

As she lies inert in the scented envelope of her bath, Ella forces her thoughts to the last weeks. What had the appearances of the Angel of Death meant? Why the constant pursuit? Was she being warned against getting too involved with Khaled? Was it possible that she felt somewhat guilty at abandoning the memory of Phil for a few weeks? Had she herself invited the Angel of Death to chaperone her on this adventure? She rejects that notion. It seems that her hopeful sojourn with a man who turned out to be a stranger had simply been a good venue, rich with possibilities, for the Angel of Death. As she floats in the cooling water, Ella comprehends that there will be more appearances, more visits, before the final rendez-vous.

The Act

Andrew McCambridge

The Act

"Acid."

"Aerosmith."

"Anaconda."

"Anaconda doesn't count!" Ricky shouts in that fat-ass voice of his.

"It's the name of my dick, Dick, and as long as it's about sex, drugs or ... rock-n-roll it counts," Frankie shoots back, but his tough-guy resolve trails off by mid-sentence.

"Looks like little Frankie over here wants a Friar Tuck — real bad." Ricky is referring to his pastime of belly-bucking his friends as does his idol in said manner on *Rocket Robin Hood*.

"Please senor, me no want trouble, hokay?" Everyone around the kitchen table laughs as Frankie flutters his eyelashes.

Like the rest of us, Frankie knows submission is the only option with Ricky. A few weeks ago, Ricky bucked me so hard my ass imprinted like a piece of shrapnel on my basement wall. We covered the crime scene with a "Never Mind the Bullocks" Sex Pistols poster to save me from my old man. Ricky's defence, "I was bored," but I knew he was trying to impress Geneviève, my girlfriend, who was in hysterics as she dislodged me. As for me, I was furious, but I knew better than to fight back. Even my older brother, The Cube, would need a few minutes to grind Ricky's pudgy cheeks into the carpet with his torture of choice – the face wash.

"Keep going!"

"Air Supply."

"I told you Dorfman was gay!"

"AC-DC"

"Alcohol."

Manuela's turn. She inhales her cigarette softly and the collective male gaze wills her to speak of sex.

"Aaa-row-zull." Her bee-stung, ruby lips stream cloudy smoke against the tacky orange wallpaper. And then, sweet silence...at least for a moment.

"ME LIKEY!" erupts Dorfman, practically salivating.

"Franchement! Can you keep it in your pants for more than two seconds?" Judging by her perma-grin, Geneviève's protest is not convincing.

"I think I can handle him," says Manuela, taking another drag from her cigarette without looking over at Geneviève. "I've seen worse."

Manuela's been out of high school two years now and she's different from the other girls at the party. And it's not just because she's older. Even as a kid skipping rope in the park or just bouncing along on her banana seat bike, Manuela could stop the most epic street hockey game just like that, but none of us ever had the balls to so much as talk to her. And now, she's got a luscious little pooper; she's what the boys and I like to call a pocket-rocket — a short girl with a juicy ass just begging to explode out of her jeans.

"It's your turn, Pretty-Boy," comes a random voice at the table.

Alpha, affair, adultery. Think dammit!

"Speak or drink!"

Anal-Anal-ANAL!!! No — too much!!!

"Uuh-Aardvark," I blurt out without thinking.

"Drink up, loser!" orders Ricky, his voice bellowing above Prince singing about a raspberry beret and a secluded farm.

"Why? It starts with an A and it's sexual!"

"Oh really?" Manuela lifts a coquettish brow.

"Sure. The long nose, the Gene Simmons tongue. The insatiable appetite.... Like me."

She giggles.

"Calme-toi, Pretty-Boy!" says Geneviève, who has circled behind me to massage my neck.

"Yes, master!"

"Keep it up with that mouth, Aidan!" From the mirror on the fridge door, I see her behind me smiling tightly as she takes a swig of my Molson without giving it back.

Beaming now at Manuela, I give a what-can-you-do shrug.

"She beats me 'cause she loves me." I'm suddenly aware of how light my head feels and I chuckle as though I'd swallowed a parakeet. Manuela cackles, then covers her mouth sheepishly. The eye-contact brings an even deeper high. The buzz feels electric...

"Écoute-moi bien, Pretty-Boy." Geneviève's voice snaps me awake as she squishes my Broncos cap backwards on my head. "You're gonna get a good old fashioned spanking when I get you home tonight!"

I peak at my reflection in the fridge mirror — my ears are popping out sideways and the zit on my forehead bursts through the opening of the cap's back closure. My already red face reddens even more.

*

I got my first bit of action with Geneviève outside the shopping mall where we hung out after school. "Shut up and kiss me, Aidan," she interrupted, as I was fumbling through my would-you-be-my-prom-date speech.

That was back in June, just before we graduated high school, and the gods were smiling upon me. In cheesy teen-movie fashion, some jock named Steve had stolen her virginity after just two weeks of dating — then never called her back. They did the deed late one night on the deck of her in-ground pool right next to the fence where her parents had hung the Snow White arm floats she wore as a baby girl. When I pointed out the irony, she slapped me good and hard. That was one beating I deserved.

I always had the hots for Geneviève, a curly redhead way out of my league, or so I thought. But now she too needed a last-minute prom date, and I could always make her laugh on our way-too-short walks home from school.

"One thing," she insisted, after saying yes. "No white boy robot dance on the dance floor." Her big eyes were smiling gently.

"You love the robot! *Domo arigato, Mr. Roboto. DOMO-domo. DOMO-domo!*"

"Mon dieu! It's gonna take months to turn Pretty-Boy into Sexy-Beast?"

The make-out lasted a good five minutes because our bus was stuck at a traffic light. When I anxiously caressed her cheek, she pulled my hand away. "Slow down, Aidan." And so I did. For a while anyway.

Geneviève and I lazed away the summer in my parents' basement, puffing Du Mauriers out a side window, playing "War" on the bed in the adjoining den and howling when my friends and I re-enacted Monty Python skits we'd memorize to impress her. For her birthday in July, I bought her a $90 Victorian-style perfume bottle I had found in an antique store. I used the little money I had made at the Royal Montreal Golf Club serving rich Anglos — the butt of hilarious curses by Geneviève's Québécois father in his fractured English — "Me, I'm not go down der with golf club, hostie. Non! I bring hockey stick and smash their têtes carées like this. CLACK! CLACK! CLACK! Now I have de power!"

"Now pay attention!" I had said, sitting across from her on my worn out basement sofa. "You stick the perfume under this elegant hoop dress, squeeze her chunky butt, and poof — she sprays the sweetest smells. Voilà, ma chérie! The perfect perfume orgasm."

"Don't act silly because you did something sweet." Geneviève kissed me hard, with a little tongue action. "Je t'aime, Aidan."

I thought I loved her too, especially since on that same July afternoon I got to touch her breasts for the first time. While my parents were ranting in the kitchen upstairs about the high cost of living — 'cause of the wicked GST, I was ecstatic at the fair price for an I-love-you and several minutes of blessed breast-squeezing.

But the thrill of crossing that heavenly threshold isn't doing it for me anymore. I was being patient and all, but a couple weeks back, just before we started college, I told her I wouldn't stand for it if she couldn't tell me when we would have sex, or ..."deeper intimacy" — a term Dorfman told me to use with a sensitive chick like Geneviève.

"Are you asking me to punch a time clock?" she screamed. "That's exactly what Steve did!"

I apologized immediately, but it's become harder to deal with this loser feeling that Pretty-Boy is playing second fiddle to a muscle-bound jerk, who just had to snap his finger and...

The sexual exploits of my brother don't help much either. In stark contrast to the deeper connections I've been forging with my girlfriend stands Carl, the Cube, who has turned that den, where Geneviève and I play our silly card games, into a porn palace. In fact, one night while my buddies and I were giggling at naked boobies on Nuit Bleu, he escorted his latest girl downstairs, winked at the lot of us, and headed straight for his secluded lair.

Frankie's pupils inflated — POOF! — like Jiffy Pop. "They're gonna fuck! I know it!"

"Let's go watch around back!" suggested Dorfman, referring to the open doorway to the den through the back basement.

The three of us retreated at least five times as we approached the archway — one of us would nervously giggle in anticipation of live sex. When Ricky pushed horny-Dorfy into the room, snorting snot shot out Frankie's nose. We howled.

The Cube erupted through the doorway like a colossal WWF

wrestler in tighty-whities, tossing us across the room like ragdolls. He saved the worst face wash for me.

"Tell me, Puke." He scrubbed my face into the carpet as he grimaced sadistically under his brush cut. "What happens when you laugh with that smart-ass mouth of yours? ... Say it!"

"Aah! I ...cry — I cry!"

"Louder!"

"I CRYYY!"

"That's right! Like you're doing right now, yafucken baby!" Then he swaggered back to the den cursing the walls. "No wonder the rat hasn't gotten his dinky stinky. Wasting his time talking girly-talk and watching others fuck. Grow some balls!"

The Cube's brutality was no surprise — just another shit-kicking in a long history of shit-kickings. But what did surprise me was my friends' peculiar reaction.

"Why don't you ever fight back?" asked Frankie, rubbing his sore neck.

"I didn't give in, and he barely touched me," boasted Ricky.

"If anyone says another word I'll lose it! My brother's an asshole — end of story!"

"Yeah, but he's cool!" said Ricky, not so much as recognizing my threat.

"Let's go tell Geneviève the Cube kicked our sorry asses!" trumpeted Frankie.

"By the way," giggled Dorfman, as I closed the door to the basement, "her nipples shot out like rockets! I bet they're bigger than Pretty Boy's boner."

"Shut up! He'll hear you!"

*

The sweet arousal around the kitchen table has been replaced by threatening stillness. A few minutes ago Manuela's boyfriend had crashed the party, squishing himself down beside her. All the while his eyes tunnelled in on me, causing my guts to twist like chicken wire. He must have heard me flirting with her.

"I'd cover up that zit on your forehead there, guy," he says, pointing at the spot. "Or better yet, pop that, that ... travesty!" I'm not sure if the others are giggling because they're as nervous as I am, or if they actually think this jerk's funny.

"You should see the one on my ass!" I counter.

Manuela laughs louder than the rest. Her boyfriend smirks in spite of himself, then, out of nowhere, starts shaking his stubby head into her chest. Manuela is as stunned as the rest of us when he snarls like some crazed animal, grinding his cheek into her lap.

"Stop it!" she protests mildly, rubbing his short hair with both hands.

What does she see in this guy? His head's too small for his buff frame and his bushy eyebrows shoot out like prickly burrs across his nose.

"And enough silliness from you, Aidan." Geneviève lifts her chin with mock-pride. "My Pretty Boy's got a sexy, pimple-free ass, thank you very much!"

"You don't say!" Manuela pushes her guy away, plopping her elbows on the table with her cheeks in her palms. Her exaggerated interest makes me think she's more annoyed with this loser than interested in me.

"You're talking about little boy over here?" Manuela's boyfriend looks at the girls in sarcastic shock. "Out with it, kid. Any pubes yet?"

"Uhh ... Does peach fuzz count?"

No one is laughing now. My neck prickles with sweat and my foot won't stop tapping the floor.

"Good one!" He says threateningly, rising up to scoop peanuts from the bowl in front of me.

"Be nice!" Manuela says, rubbing his chest.

"Yo, guy! The only one who gets to torment Pretty-Boy at this party is me." Ricky has always stood up for me since grade school.

"I ain't talking to you, lard-ass," he shoots back, giving Ricky the stare down. "And I've got a few friends here who'll make sure it stays that way." He tilts his head towards his three cronies leaning against the far wall; by the way they're dressed, the white T-shirts, black Levis and black Docs, we know instantly they're Rebels — the closest thing to a gang our corner of suburbia has manufactured. I say manufactured because most of the time Average Joes', like me, brush them off as middle-class wannabes. But now isn't one of those times.

"Il n'a rien fait, so get lost, poser," yells Geneviève.

"So now your girlfriend defends you. But I guess she's not the bitch in that relationship, is she?"

"That's why they call him Pretty Boy," jibes the greaser friend with biceps bulging from his folded arms. The collective snicker makes my blood boil before I consider the churning in my stomach. For this moment, I don't care what happens to me.

"Why is it James Dean wannabes always act like jerks?" I stab right back at him.

"How is it that a gaggle-fuck like you has a girlfriend in the first place?"

"Do mommy and daddy just not understand the pain, Mono-brow?" I wave my fists in front of my chest with feigned angst.

"You're the preppy, faggot."

"It's a simple equation really. Insecure punk, plus rebel clothing, equals complete asshole." I count it out with my fingers: one-two-three. The table is mine.

Manuela is alert and intrigued, turning her head back and forth from me to him like she's watching some tennis rally. And now, Mono-brow is seething; the enflamed muscles on his face are twitching as he burns me with his stare. The only sound I hear — the pulse of air firing out his nostrils.

"That kinda talk's gonna make me put you in your place." Mono-brow steps up from the other side of the table, waving his hands down towards his crotch — a dancing motion. "Let's do it!"

I clench the beer in my hand, wanting to hurl it in his ugly face, but ... I can't. A private thrashing in my basement is humiliating enough; a public beating with the screaming and the tears, in front of all these girls — too mortifying.

"You wish!" I retort desperately, not moving.

"Tsss! It's all just talk with you, eh, joker."

"You promised no more of this," Manuela pleads, wrapping her arms around his chest. "Remember?"

Mono-brow pushes her aside and mutters "Goddammit" to the wall. Composing himself, he focuses back in on me. "That's too bad for you, Pretty Boy. A good ass-kicking would knock some sense into you ...Let's get out of here, boys."

"You're really gonna let this punk talk to you like that?" asks the same crony who insulted me before.

"I said we're outta here. Let these queers jerk each other off."

The Rebels strut to the doorway like outlaws with Manuela close behind.

Mono-Brow jerks his head back at me. "Soon, Pretty Boy."

For the first time I notice all the penetrating eyes drilling in at me from the archway.

"Don't let them get to you, Aidan. Rebel punks is all," says Dorfman.

"No doubt." I know my voice will crack if I say another word, so I don't.

"He's right about the pretty thing though," says Frankie. "Can I jerk you off now?"

I muster up a giggle as he grabs my shoulder and Geneviève squeezes my hand under the table. "It's time we leave this place," she murmurs.

Neither gesture stops that drowning feeling.

*

The car shrieks through the shadowy side-streets. The glaring lights behind us slash through the darkness — a rifle steadying on its target. Geneviève screams a commanding "shut up!" over the panicky voices telling her what to do as she weaves through the empty suburban maze. We dip below rows of townhouses beneath Saint-Thomas Church, where I used to kill the Cube with my dirty church songs. *"This is my boner, given for your freedom. These are my balls which I shed for all mankind."*

We swerve around a corner and hit an enormous pothole — BOOM — my head smacks the roof so hard my chin squishes into my chest. Wiry branches reach into the open passenger-side windows and scratch me in the backseat as we swing within a hair of the fence blocking Thorndale Elementary School, where Ricky used to reign supreme at "King of the Mountain" on the giant snow hill.

I turn my head over my shoulder to catch a glimpse of the blazing yellow eyes zeroing in on our tail. THWACK! My ear crashes down on my shoulder and burning needles stab up and down my neck.

"They could kill us!" shouts Ricky, who never looks scared.

We speed down the steep hill on Rolland Street, where the Cube once gripped the back bumper of my elementary school bus and hitched down the snow-covered street in his unlaced Kodiaks. Snow jetted into the air as he glided triumphantly into a snow bank at the bottom. I can still remember the kids running down the street to applaud him as my bus turned out of sight.

And it hits me. I give Geneviève the order. "Drive to my place. My parents are away. The Cube'll have his way with these assholes."

"The Cube'll kill 'em!" crows Dorfman.

"Yeah, and rape us for good measure" says Frankie, without getting his customary laugh.

I suddenly realize I have Geneviève's softball equipment on my lap. I jam it into the hatchback trunk behind me as we veer on to King Street. I take a deep breath and brace myself for a fight I know we can win.

*

Geneviève screeches to a halt in front of Aidan's parent's house, and they sprint past the Cube's convertible on the driveway. He unlocks the front door and ushers his four friends into the hallway: Frankie and Dorfman, then Ricky, and, finally, his girlfriend — *enough with the chick panic! Move your ass, girl!*

Mono-brow's Eldorado shark-jaws over the curb tearing at the grass and jerks to a stop. His three cronies crawl out slowly — Mono-brow a stride ahead as they advance in unison. Giant stick men. But he senses apprehension in their procession and he feels something unexpected – composure.

Pushing Geneviève inside, Aidan pulls the front door closed without entering. He exhales evenly; she is safe now. He steps down the paved stairs with deliberate calm and faces Mono-brow. *You see that car on the driveway? It belongs to my brother, and he's gonna destroy you!* Their quiet voices mutter something incoherent. When their dark bodies are within five feet, they charge. He swings back recklessly.

His Broncos hat flies off his head as his face gets smothered in someone's stomach. Their shapeless forms wrestle him to the grass. Thick fingers scratch his scalp and clamp into his long hair. Aidan opens his eyes — Mono-brow's burning pupils block out the horizon as his hairy knuckles thunder down on his cracking face again and again and again. He's crying furiously. Absolute terror — not from the pounding — he's too alive to feel it. Total vulnerability is driving his panic. But he somehow composes himself enough to scream with everything he has. "CARL, HELP ME!"

A heavy body crashes on the scrum, driving Aidan's head into the dirt, steamrolling over him and setting him free. He scrambles away from the grunting voices and sees Ricky lumbering his hefty frame off the ground. "Really tough, Mono-brow," says Ricky, brushing the dirt from his shirt. "Four of you against one, asshole," he adds, stepping back to the center of a wall of Geneviève, Dorfman and Frankie, now shielding him from Mono-brow. He scans the lawn and confirms his suspicion — the Cube is nowhere to be seen.

"We don't back down from nobody, do we, boys?" yells Mono-brow, as an unseen crony shoves Dorfman, driving him back a good five feet. From the small opening in the protective line Aidan glimpses Geneviève slapping frantically at Mono-brow's chest. "Quit it with this macho bullshit! He's already beaten!"

He tries to lift himself up, but an acid migraine weighs him down, blurring his vision. He keeps blinking to refocus, but the scene wilts to slow-motion.

"Whoaaaaa! I ...wooon't... hit... a ...girrrl!" lulls Mono-brow's voice, his waving palms protesting. He lifts his chin beyond Geneviève and he zeroes in on Aidan, a wounded animal whimpering in the grass. "I'm getting tired of your games, Pretty Boy. When are you gonna face me like a man?"

Aidan reacts slowly. Spitting bloody dirt from his mouth, he draws himself up — eyes locked on Mono-brow. A surging energy twitches his muscles; a swelling force burning faster and faster expresses itself in his torrid grunts. He approaches Mono-brow; his tunnel vision drawing a perfect bead on his tormentor. He moves past his friends, who, like the cronies, seem paralyzed, silenced by the vicious growls pumping from his lungs. His sharp fingers claw at Mono-brow's throat and hurl him to the ground. His forehead presses down on Mono-brow's eyes and he can feel his own tears between their squished cheeks. He is snarling — nonsensical.

He jerks his neck back and crashes his head down on Mono-brow like a cinder block. "Now I'm smashing your ugly face in, you fucking puke." Mono-brow's arms slacken after three head-butts. But Aidan cannot relent just yet. He jams his knees into Mono-brow's arm sockets turned on by his victim's horrific shrieking. "Now I'm scratching your eyeballs out, rat. Look who's crying now!"

His senses feet encroaching from behind. He shoots a pointed finger over his shoulder. "Back the fuck away!" When he turns his head to look, Ricky is blocking Geneviève from getting any closer.

"STOP, AIDAN! YOU'RE KILLING HIM!" He will never forget how afraid she is when their eyes lock for that instant.

Aidan slithers off the ragged body beneath him, marches past his friends and picks his cap up off the paved walkway. Geneviève is wailing into Ricky's chest while the others console her. Behind them Mono-brow's head droops like a scarecrow as his cronies lift him from the ground. *Give that rat one last reminder.* Aidan charges forward and punts him between the legs as hard as he possibly can. Mono-brow falls face-first, but his friends do nothing. He flashes a lizard smile at the greaser friend, the one who taunted him at the party. "I don't hear you calling me Pretty Boy now, do I?" He leans in until their foreheads touch. "Do I, pussy?" He will never forget the boy's frozen fear.

He can't distinguish the shadowy neighbours whispering at the edge of the darkened sidewalk, but he will remember their look — the witnesses to the act.

He enters his house and looks into the window-pane mirror at the entrance. In the top frames mud has curdled with the strands of black hair underneath a ball cap. He follows the blood dripping down in each partition from the two purple eyelids — swollen eyelids all but sealed shut. He breaks free from the initial terror of not recognizing this fractured self squinting back at him. He shoots back a lightning glare then smiles at his reflection beneath inflated lips. *I could tear you apart!*

He is happy his brother wasn't home.

*

I was anxious to get away from the bus stop where Geneviève interrupted our first kiss a few months back. It's still hard for me to believe we only started college two months ago... Everything is different now.

It's been three weeks since the act.

I walk to the back of the bus coolly, pretending not to notice the annoying old lady stealing glances at my still-bruised face, and sit myself down on the back bench.

I know Geneviève and the guys are in the mall right now playing "Asshole" in the food-court just like we always do after afternoon lectures. I wouldn't say I miss it all that much; the same boring routine every day: Dorfman drooling at every single tit bouncing by, Frankie jumping around the food court like a dancing fool, and Ricky putting me down, just hoping Geneviève'll notice. But, there were a few good moments... Like the time Frankie dared me to lob a bunch of jujubes into the vat of chilli behind the Taco Bravo stand. The memory of that old French lady and her perplexed "Comment?" as she noticed a bloody-red gummy bear on her spoon, and how we all turtled under the table... It was pretty funny stuff! But strangely, what's stayed with me the most is how eagerly that old lady joined in our laughter once she figured us out. "Amusez-vous, les jeunes. Ce sont les meilleurs moments de vos vie." That was only a few weeks ago — amazing how quickly things change.

I tap my fingers in a steady beat — tap-tap-tap — against the filthy bus window. A bunch of kids across the street are playing soccer-baseball in a playground. I gnaw at an itch on my upper lip.

"Maybe I should go out with him then! At least he gives a shit!" That's what Geneviève cried out in our fight last week; an embarrassing shouting match she started in the school cafeteria. Man, did she ever love fighting in public like that; and the more people watching, the better. What bugged me the most was how she then tried to play the victim, just staring at her finger picking the rotted corner on her side of the table.

"Then go out with him. It'll be no surprise to me," I finally replied, refusing to play into her bullshit. "I mean, you jumped right into my arms as soon as you left Steve."

"Will you look at yourself in the mirror, Aidan?" She dangled her fingers above her shoulders mockingly. "Regardez-moi, tout le monde! I'm a real big-shot now with my big black eyes and fat lip."

"At least I'm no phony like my so-called friend. Waiting like a vulture to pounce on my leftovers."

"So now I'm your leftovers?"

"You tell that rat that if I see him on the street, he better cross to the other side, or I swear I'll bite his fucking nose off."

When I sprung up to leave, I accidentally pushed the table a little harder than expected and it rammed her in the gut. Her loud *ugh!* was totally exaggerated though, but I still felt bad about it. I thought of turning back to apologize, but I didn't. That was the last time we spoke.

But not everything has gone sour since the act. The wide-eyed interest from the guys on campus — *those shiners are totally sick, boy!* – the strange compliments from sassy girls — *your scars are so ... ugly-sexy!*

And the Cube ... With a cooler full of beer and his friends over to watch the Montreal Canadiens home opener last week, they got into a big argument over who would have won the disrupted fight between hulking Flyer goalie Ron Hextall and our scrappy Hab Chris Chelios in the war-like 1989 conference finals.

"No contest!" shouted George, a scraggy mullet-head in a worn-out lumberjack shirt. "Chelios is 180 pounds soaking wet and Hextall's a monster."

"PRETTY BOY — BEER — NOW!" ordered the Cube with a snap of his fingers as was his custom on hockey nights.

"Don't call me that!" I shot back. My scars were almost healed by then.

"Well, lookie-here," said George. "Pretty Boy popped his cherry and now he thinks he can mouth off to the Cube."

"Now-now, George. I'll get my own beer for a change."

Could it be this simple? I couldn't help thinking the guys were right all along about my brother. I triumphantly leaned my head back on the couch as the Cube bent forward to open that damn cooler himself. But within a second I felt a Budweiser can smack off my chest, exploding against the wall. I knew it! That complete prick would never let up! I jumped up instinctively ready to tear him apart once and for all when I saw the Cube ... smiling.

"And besides, George," said the Cube in an unfamiliar tone. "I'd watch it if I were you. Tough Guy over here's got his own move now to rival my face wash. It's called the Aidan head-butt!"

Dishing back a wry smirk, I grabbed the beer spurting wildly on the carpet and turned to that scrawny weakling. "And you're wrong about that Hextall thing too, Georgie-boy. Chelios is the most tenacious little fucker you'll ever see!"

"Heyyy yooou!" I feel a light punch on my arm that startles me out of these musings. I turn my head from the bus window to see who it is. Manuela sits herself down cross-legged on the empty seat beside me. "Your scars are healing nicely."

"She beats me 'cause she loves me, remember?" Manuela's face is as pretty as always, but she's a little thinner than I remember.

Brushing her dark bangs to the side, she reveals an excited smile. "Can I touch it?"

"As long as you don't confuse sex with love."

"I'm not asking to touch that, you perv... This." She presses her index finger firmly on the big scar below my right eye. "Ick! It's so disgusting," she protests, without removing her finger.

I wince and pull her hand away firmly.

"Come on! You can take it, Pretty Boy!... One thing though." She takes a compact mirror from her backpack and dabbles makeup on my cheek. "You need to get rid of this ugly pink splotch. It draws too much attention ... Now. Take a look."

I angle the mirror down slowly — down from the blood stains on the inner panel of my Broncos cap, past the yellow shiners under my bright blue eyes, to the scar that inflates my upper lip just enough for others to notice. I rub out the foundation abruptly. "Let 'em look. I don't care what people think."

"Suuure you don't!" Manuela's haughty smile makes me want to fuck her.

Without warning, she removes my cap and skips to the side exit as the bus comes to her stop. "Call me if you want your hat back."

"Wait! I don't have your number."

"You're an aardvark, remember?" She slants an elegant shoulder back at me as she steps out. "Sniff around with that long nose of yours until you find it."

*

. I got my Broncos cap back and then some. I still remember Manuela laughing as we were lying down on Westminster Hill way past midnight. She said I was no longer an aardvark — from now on she would call me a bucking-bronco. "Please do," I insisted. "And pass the word on to all your dirty friends."

She punched my arm with a clumsy grin, "You jerk!" I noticed the light frost rising from her lips before she lay her head back down on my chest.

After my second orgasm we got dressed and I walked her home, both of us bantering playfully along the way.

I never called her back.

Night Out

Sabine Walser

Night Out

"What time is the babysitter coming?" Clyde asks Alexandra.

"Usual time."

"What, 7?"

"Yes, 7. Doesn't she always come at 7?" she asks.

"Relax, I just wasn't sure." Clyde comes up behind her as she is in the process of pouring the kids' bath, and leans over her back, cupping her breasts. Alexandra stumbles. "Clyyyyde, I'm about to fall," she says, shaking him off.

"Are you going to be this sour all night?"

"I'm not *sour*." She gets up, her face red from bending over the tub. "Can you call the kids, please? And would you mind making them dinner?"

"Do we have any eggs?"

"Didn't you buy some today?"

"Oh yeah, I forgot." He makes a face like *silly me*, only this time she catches him at it. It's an expression she recognizes.

In her son's room, she collects the books left on the floor and crams them into the overstuffed bookcase, tosses the scattered cars into the car bin, the plastic dinosaurs into the dinosaur bin. Then she goes into Molly's room to get her pj's from the crib.

During bath time, Linus and Molly shriek and splash Alexandra, who laughs and puts her hands on their wet little bodies: chubby, soapy, delicious. Drying the kids, Alexandra kisses Molly's belly and her pudgy cheeks with a rapacious hunger, awed at how delightful she is with towel dried hair; Linus's towel becomes a superhero cape and he jumps on her, shouting "Superman!" Alexandra scoops him in her arms and kisses his neck. As she gets their pajamas on, the kids shout-squeal-squirm-stumble, making it difficult for her to close the snaps: she holds each one down firmly.

Once the kids are downstairs, she feels tremendous relief at the silence and stillness of the bathroom, followed by shame that the chaos of her children disquiets her, that she can't wait to be rid of them for the evening.

After a quick hot shower, she smears lotion all over and puts on her (and Clyde's) favorite black lacy underwear. Putting on the thong makes her horny as she anticipates fun, drunken, post night-out sex. She and Clyde had wanted to make love during nap time, but Linus hadn't slept. When they kissed while Linus was watching *The Lion King*, their lips had quickly gotten hot and Clyde had whispered, "Just wait until tonight..." Thursday night's love making had been so passionate and satisfying; they had spoken frequently about wanting a repeat performance, like teenagers discovering first orgasms. Their hunger was probably due to the dry spell – it had been a few weeks. *Four and a half, to be exact. But who's counting?* Alexandra scowls at her fat and the stretch marks on her soft stomach, annoyed and disgusted with the bulges around the thong. The underwear looks nothing like the model in the Victoria Secret catalogue. *Thank God I'm still nursing.* The bra serves its purpose, pushing up and in in the right places, magically, mercifully, transforming udders into cleavage.

While Clyde plays Tickle Monster with the kids, she finishes getting ready: she puts on an ivory wrap-around dress; it doesn't hide her thick hips, but it also doesn't hide her cleavage. She spends considerable effort getting her hair into a low chignon and when finally she is done, she calls Clyde to bring the kids to bed.

She settles with Molly in the rocking chair to nurse: Molly opens widely, puts her little fist on Alexandra's breast and nestles in. She drinks sleepily, every now and then popping off to smile at Alexandra or to grab her necklace. Alexandra closes her eyes and relaxes deeply, treasuring this effortless symbiosis, somehow easier and purer than sex. When Molly finishes, Alexandra kisses her warm velvetplump cheeks, lingering and relishing the buttery baby fat. "Good night, my sweet. I love you, sleep well." She starts the music box, turns off the light and gently shuts the door.

"Let's read a Richard Scarry book," she suggests to Linus. After the story, she kisses Linus's belly while blowing out her cheeks, producing loud farting sounds which elicit screams and giggles from Linus. *That was stupid of me.* She smoothes his forehead and strokes his cheeks, awed by his beauty, his clear blue eyes, his mop of blond hair, his perfect lips. She tucks his gingham duvet under his chin and kisses each cheek, inhaling the smell of baby shampoo.

"Good night, my sweet, I love you. Sleep well." She turns to go, dreading what is about to come.

Linus sits up. "Mummy, lie down with me."

Alexandra sighs. "No, Linus. It's time to go to sleep."

"No! Lie down!! I'm scared."

"There's nothing to be scared of. Go to sleep." Linus starts crying, loudly. She caves.

"Okay, but only for five minutes, and then I'm going. Okay?"

"Okay." Linus cuddles his stuffed alligator, nuzzles against her, then sleepily turns on his side. Alexandra yanks at her dress so as not to wrinkle it and instead flattens her chignon; her thong gives her a tight wedgie. The resentment starts building.

She rises suddenly. "Ok, honey, I'm going now. I'll be downstairs and Karen is coming in about 20 minutes."

The stern tone backfires, and Linus becomes frantic. "No, Mummy, stay with me!! Sleep with me!"

"Shhh. You're okay. Daddy and I aren't leaving yet. It's bed time. *Good night*."

"No!! Stay with me!!" Linus shouts and starts pulling on her dress.

The crying provokes her anger, his neediness strangles her. "Linus, go to sleep!" She snatches her dress out of his little grip and storms out the room.

Linus wails, "Mummy, I need you! Come back! Mummy! Mummy! Mummy!"

Stomping down the stairs, Alexandra pulls her hair down. "He has to learn to sleep by himself," she hisses at Clyde.

"He will when he's ready. He's scared to be alone. It's just a phase." Clyde climbs the stairs to Linus's room.

*

"He's asleep," Clyde says as he enters the kitchen where Alexandra is scrubbing the pan.

Alexandra turns around. Clyde is wearing the slightly shiny, dark purple, wide collared shirt that he bought in New York years ago; they'd had a fight about it then.

She thought, coupled with his neat haircut and his slim physique that the shirt made him look gay. Clyde didn't care, but she thought that if he looked gay, clearly that was a statement about her and her sexuality, *their* sexuality. People would assume they didn't have a wild and crazy sex life. Besides, she'd already had one lover who turned out to be gay; she couldn't handle two. Clyde had pursed his lips at the time and wouldn't engage in the argument, staying silent and pissed off.

She turns back to her pan, scrubbing harder. Seeing Clyde in that shirt, her amorous, X-rated fantasies for the end of their evening dissolve. *Don't say anything*. She bites her lower lip and knits her brow scouring the pan, while the S.O.S. pad gets clogged with wet egg crumbs. *Don't say anything*.

"Do you want a drink?" Clyde asks

"No thanks....Nice shirt," she says. Clyde says nothing. She forges on. "Are you really going to wear that?"

"What's wrong with it?"

"Nothing."

"Then why'd you ask?"

"Never mind," she says.

"Alexandra..."

"I said, never mind."

"What?"

"It's just not my favorite shirt.... It's tacky.... Can't you change?" She speaks harshly, *tacky* comes out with extra zeal. Clyde looks at her, miffed.

"I'm not changing. I like this shirt."

"Yeah, but it's an ugly shirt. It makes you look pale." She presses on. "Why can't you change? You have so many other nice shirts." The shirt doesn't match her image of them: a married couple still deeply in love, who look good, and despite having two small children, interrupted sleep and a messy house still do it. The shirt, coupled with Alexandra's busty dress, makes them look desperate: it suggests that having kids, looking good, going out, keeping it all together is astounding effort.

"God, you're petty."

"Maybe I am. But that shirt just makes you look like a geek!" Her voice rises, petulant.

"So...So what if I look like a geek? Christ, Alexandra. What's going on here?"

"What do you mean, *'what's going on?'*? Nothing's going on. I just hate that shirt. I hate how it makes you look."

Clyde takes a sip of his Scotch, looks at her with tight lips, shakes his head and walks out of the kitchen. The silent shake of his head inflames her shame. She takes refuge by putting the dishes away, wiping the table and counter, even sweeping the floor — tasks she usually avoids. She then carefully wraps the scarf for Abigail, adding two different ribbons for a pretty effect. Eventually, she enters the living room where she finds Clyde reading the travel section. The silence is palpable.

"I'm sorry...Clyde, I'm sorry...." She dumps the Lego pieces into the box. Taking small sips of Scotch, Clyde gives a spiteful laugh and keeps reading.

"Clyde, I'm sorry. I know you're not a geek."

He doesn't look up. "I'm relieved."

"You're mad, aren't you?"

"I just don't understand why you made such a big deal of it."

"I didn't make a big deal. I just said I didn't like it."

"No, you didn't *just* say you didn't like it. Your tone was mean — it's all in the delivery, Alexandra." Whenever he uses her name like that she feels especially small.

"I know. I just wanted us to look good together.... Of course it doesn't matter what shirt you wear. I was being really stupid. I'm sorry." She sits down next to him and runs her hands through his long, thick, black, wavy hair. She begins kissing him, but Clyde stiffens, and his lips stay tense; he offers only small, cold, hard pecks. "I'm *sorry*," she repeats. "Are you mad?"

"I'm not mad, just hurt." He gets up to let Karen in.

Fuck. Why can't you be mad, instead of hurt?

*

The French bistro, with its uneven wooden floors, white table cloths and red lanterns, is full and lively; Paolo Conte is crooning from the speakers: *"It's wonderful, It's wonderful, It's wonderful, Good luck my baby"*. Their friends are at a large table in the back.

"Happy birthday, Abigail. You look gorgeous," Alexandra lies. Abigail is taller and thinner than Alexandra, but her short stringy blond hair and black suit offers an androgynous look that doesn't appeal, she thinks.

"Thanks, honey. So do you. Check out that dress, you look amazing." Alexandra smiles demurely and mumbles thank you, feeling a mixture of victory (she knows she looks better than Abigail) and shame (Abigail clearly isn't threatened, which of course defeats Alexandra's sense of victory). Alexandra turns to Sean, who gives her warm kisses on each cheek and also mentions her dress. She flushes: red hives sprout on her chest, her cheeks grow red, her lips too. She begins to glow, but any more redness and she'll look obscene.

Alexandra and Clyde say hello to the other couples. As they figure out where to sit, a man arrives who goes straight to Abigail, slowly hugs her, and seductively whispers something in her ear. He then shakes Sean's hand and makes his way through the crowd introducing himself. He is tall, with green eyes, long black hair, a five o'clock shadow, big lips, an olive green cashmere scarf wrapped around his neck, and a whiff of arrogance. He glances at Alexandra and then, because he is aware that she has noticed him, ignores her as he says hello to everyone else. When he reaches her, they lock eyes and silently savor each other. He introduces himself as Mateo, from Madrid.

Alexandra confesses to her best friends, Daisy and Nina, about the shirt fight. She is honest and self-deprecating in her description of the fight – she wants to confess, to be forgiven, to be absolved. Daisy and Nina laugh and empathize. Daisy tells a similar story involving Gabriel wearing a baseball hat to her own vernissage in a swank gallery. "I mean, really, an Expos *baseball hat*?!" Nina recounts an ex-girlfriend who wore white socks and sandals – "Ewww" Daisy and Alexandra say simultaneously – and how Nina should've known it wouldn't work because of that. Alexandra feels relieved that her girlfriends understand, that maybe she is not that petty, maybe it's just a girl thing.

Mateo is sizing the three of them up, Alexandra notices. Nina's pixy hair, slim shoulders and smoky eyes have a sultry, sexy effect, but Nina pays him no attention. *One less threat.* Daisy, like Alexandra, loves to flirt, but at nine months pregnant, with a huge belly, big arms and a rosy round face to match, she exudes earthy, saintly motherhood. *Also not a threat.* She glances at Mateo, noting without the scarf around his neck he looks less like Antonio Banderas. Nonetheless, she straightens her back so her boobs don't sag, and they flirt with their eyes.

"Man, when is this baby going to come? I need to pee — again," says Daisy.

"I need to pee too," says Nina, as she gets up.

"You guys, don't leave me," Alexandra says.

"Come with us."

"No, the bathroom's tiny — there won't be room. Never mind." With no one sitting on either side of her and a plate of foie gras in front of her, Alexandra feels exposed. The pâté is silksumptuous smooth — appreciating it alone makes her feel smutty (certain creamy pleasures only seem decent if shared). She takes small, prissy bites forcing her lips to tighten and is relieved when the plate is finally empty, her indulgence sated.

Waves of laughter erupt throughout the meal. Clyde's deep voice can be heard at his end. He is doing his magic: pouring the wine and making people laugh. Nina and Daisy have returned from the bathroom, but have stopped to talk to Abigail. Daisy is explaining the home-water-birth she is planning.

Alexandra's mussels in white wine and garlic arrive. She looks to see if Daisy and Nina will return, but now Daisy is informing Abigail of her plans to cook the placenta and eat it at the baby's naming ceremony. She picks up a mussel. She inadvertently inspects it and is again surprised how it looks like female genitalia. Years ago, the first time she ate mussels the phrase "It looks exactly like a vagina!" screeched through her head. Blushing, Alexandra had reprimanded herself for seeing vagina's everywhere and tried to avoid examining them as she ate them, while only occasionally gagging. She's come a long way since then — she no longer reddens while appreciating suggestive seafood.

Mateo, whose conversation partners have ditched him, casually looks over at Alexandra, takes a big gulp of wine and swishes it in his mouth. The silence is awkward.

"How do you know Abigail?" she finally asks him.

"We met in Spain when she was studying Spanish there. We lived in the same building."

"Really?" Alexandra doesn't have a good follow up question and concentrates on picking her way through her fleshy mussels.

"How are your mussels?" he asks.

From all the wine she's been sipping in her attempt to look at ease, Alexandra's head feels full, rosy, blurry, numb. She hesitates, then answers slowly and deliberately, "Really sexy." It is the wine talking and she is now flirting out right; since Clyde is absorbed by his friends, by the attention and by the buzz of being centre stage, she feels it's safe — and only fair. "Have you ever noticed how obscene some mussels look? They're so... so... explicit, you know what I mean? Almost pornographic. They kind of make me blush... Do you want one?" She looks straight into his eyes. Mateo fiddles with his food.

"I don't like mussels, actually. We always had to eat them as kids, and I never liked them, they're too fishy — like oysters or sushi." Alexandra is disappointed that he doesn't take the bait and judges him for not liking the same food she and Clyde do.

"Oh…. How are your sweetbreads?" she asks.

"Nice."

"That's good," Alexandra answers with some coolness in her voice.

She notices his hands as he starts eating. His fingers are pale, doughy, flabby; the bones look flaccid. And his wrists are bald, unmasculine — they do not satisfy her wrist fetish. She prefers hairy, bony wrists — like Clyde's — with shirt sleeves rolled a third way up the arm. Mateo chews loudly with his mouth open and a drop of sauce remains on his chin.

Every now and then Clyde smiles at Alexandra so she realizes she has been forgiven. Her love and pride for him — for someone so attractive and sexy — surges. *He is just so handsome. Why did I care about that shirt?* She feels lucky to be able to forget the limp Mateos of the world. Clyde winks at her as he moves around the table, changing places to sit and talk with other people — though not with Alexandra. "Happy birthday" is sung to Abigail, dessert arrives, so do espressos and cognacs. It is late; everyone is giddy and drunk so the good-byes are long-winded: coats are on, but people are still talking. Alexandra yawns, ready to go home. Sean, Gabriel and Clyde huddle together, half leaning on each other, supporting Sean who is very drunk and is convincing Clyde and Gabriel to go out for another drink. It is 12:15.

"We told Karen we'd be home by 12:30," Alexandra reminds Clyde.

"Oh yeah, I forgot."

"You go on with Sean, I'll go home."

"Are you sure?"

"Yeah, yeah, go."

"No, I'll come home."

"No, really, go. *Go.*"

"You're so great." Clyde embraces her and nuzzles her neck. "I won't be long. Wait for me." He squeezes her ass. Alexandra loves hearing that because they often did leave parties separately but there was never a suggestion that the other should wait up, that sex would still happen — it was simply understood that the other person would be asleep.

"I'll wait, but don't be too late." She kisses Clyde on the lips, relieved with herself for genuinely not minding that Clyde is going out. Strutting home, she feels very mature, smug that their relationship is so balanced, infused equally with independence and intimacy.

After paying the babysitter, checking on, gazing at and admiring both kids, she settles in front of the TV to wait for Clyde. The choice boils down to "Saturday Night Live" or soft porn. In an attempt to keep her mood moist, the porn prevails. Two tanned, shiny, buffed bodies grind unconvincingly together. *How can they fuck that long?* On "Saturday Night Live" Björk wails. Back to the porn, two women are at it while a guy watches. *That's more like it.* The brunette goes down on the blond, while the man enters the brunette from behind. Alexandra swells slipperyslickwet. She squeezes her thighs, looks at the clock and wonders where Clyde is. It'd be so easy to let her fingers slip down and slither around. *No. I'll wait.* The scene ends, and Alexandra flips between Tina Fey giving the news and a rerun of Rachel and Ross dealing with parenthood. Once the choice is down to "Hockey: After Hours" and the Brat Pack movie "About Last Night," she decides to go to bed.

Brushing her teeth, she listens for sounds of the front door opening. She washes her face, pats on her expensive eye cream (does she need it yet?), pees, takes off her dress but leaves her thong and bra on, and flops into bed, her drunken buzz and horniness drying up. It's 2:00 A.M. — over an hour and a half since she's left the restaurant. Her anger starts growing. There's a knot in her stomach. She imagines Clyde at the bar, drunker, tipping back shots of Jägermeister, buying a round or two. *Will he even be able to do it?* A blackness envelops her and turns everything inside of her off. Closed. Shut. Tight. After 10 more minutes, Alexandra yanks off her underwear, pulls on her old t-shirt, and turns off the light.

The front door opens. Her pulse quickens. She listens to decipher what Clyde will do: will he go to the kitchen to pig out on leftovers because he got stoned with his friends and then stumble upstairs with bad breath? Or will he watch TV, fall asleep and stagger up at 4:00 A.M.? He does neither. He turns off all the lights and tiptoes upstairs, looks in on the kids, and then slithers into the bed. Alexandra doesn't move. Clyde spoons her, starts kissing her neck — making small groans — and his hands start teasing her. She lies heavy, pretending to be deeply asleep. He whispers, "I'm not too late, am I? Mmmmm, you smell so good, you're so warm." He plasters big fat wet kisses on her, rubbing his hard-on against her ass.

Through a fake, heavy, tired voice, she mumbles, "I'm too tired." She wants him to experience her rejection as a door slammed shut. Like a hard slap. Like a steel wall. Instead, his warm hands move up to caress her breasts.

"It's okay, you don't have to wake up. I'll do the work...," he says in between sucking her earlobe — something that usually drives her wild. Alexandra rolls onto her stomach, pulls the covers with her and says decisively, "*No.*" The door is slammed shut. Tight.

"Oh...Okay..." He unwraps himself from her, goes to the bathroom (she can't hear what he's doing, *Oh God, what if he's jerking off?*), then silently gets into bed, and lays on his back with his arm under his head, as if he's contemplating life.

Within five minutes he is snoring.

Alexandra remains motionless while a piercing scream swirls inside. *But why didn't you come home sooner!? What were you thinking: that I'd just wait up all night, twiddling my thumbs? Why did you choose your friends over me? Didn't you know that I'd go to bed? Didn't you think — as you had that second or third shot — that you were blowing your chances? You even told me to wait up! I said not to be long, and over an hour, that's long, isn't it? Not long is twenty minutes, 30 max — the bar is just around the corner.* But an hour and a half!? *Didn't you want to have sex? What was so fun at the bar? Why didn't you just come home after the first drink?*

And now he is sleeping, snoring, he doesn't seem bothered at all. If the roles were reversed, she'd feel devastated, crushed, hurt, rejected, ugly. But Clyde accepts her refusal, as if she'd just said, "Clyde, *really*, it's 2:00 A.M., I'm just too tired to play tennis right now — tomorrow maybe." If Alexandra is turned on, but Clyde isn't, she feels like a mare in heat, rubbing against a wooden post, wondering where her stallion is. But Clyde doesn't feel ashamed and doesn't make her feel badly or start a pissy argument; he just says with accepted resignation okay, and goes to sleep.

But why'd you give up so easily? Aren't you turned on? Don't you need or want release? Are you just too drunk to fuck?

She eventually falls asleep with a knit brow, the creases between her eyebrows becoming embedded.

*

At 7:30 A.M., Molly throws her stuffed animals out of the crib, shrieking; Linus soon after jumps out of bed and runs into his parents' bedroom to snuggle between them. Alexandra gets Molly and comes back to bed to nurse her. Molly suckles for a few minutes but is more interested in playing with Linus, who climbs onto Clyde's back, bouncing up and down. When Clyde farts, Linus shouts, "Daddy farted! Daddy farted!" Alexandra rolls over. As Clyde tickles the kids, they scream and tumble. Linus bumps his elbow into Alexandra's back. "Ow!" she shouts. "Guys get off me! I'm trying to sleep." Linus and Molly keep jumping around, tripping, falling, laughing. "Ok, that's enough! If you want to jump on a bed, go jump on Linus's bed. This is the quiet bed. I need to sleep," Alexandra says. Clyde yawns, heaves himself up and scoops Molly in his arms.

"Let's go, guys. Let's let Mummy sleep. Who wants pancakes for breakfast?" he asks.

"Me! Me!" Linus shouts. She overhears Clyde in Molly's room, making her laugh as he changes her diaper. On the way downstairs, Linus whispers loudly "Molly! Shhhhhhhh…Mummy's sleeping."

She wakes up an hour later, with a headache and a heavy mood and smells coffee. On TV, Linus is bouncing along to Simba singing "I just can't wait to be king." Molly is playing with blocks and Clyde is in the kitchen reading the paper.

"Hey, gorgeous. Can I get you a coffee?"

"It's okay, I'll get it." Her tone is drab, her face dull. Out of the oven, Clyde pulls a plate with four thick blueberry-flaxseed pancakes which he sets in front of Alexandra. "Thank you," she mumbles. She smothers them in butter and maple syrup and starts eating. But she doesn't start chatting about last night: about how fun it was, wasn't it?; what was he talking about at his end of the table?; did he know that Nina had a new girlfriend?; how Daisy was getting so big; how Abigail was just so great, she's so glad they've become close friends, didn't he think so too?, Sean is great too, didn't he think so too? She doesn't say a word. Her face looks sour, ratty, cranky — grey.

"What's wrong?"

"Nothing."

"Yes, it is. What's up?"

"Nothing's wrong!" Then she blurts out, faltering: "Last night…"

"You were fast asleep when I came home…"

"No, I wasn't. I was awake…"

"You were?"

"I was just so mad at you for not coming home…"

"But you said I could go."

"I know I did, but…why did you stay out so late? You even told me to wait up; I thought you'd be back in, like, half an hour."

"I'm sorry. I didn't know it was so late — we lost track of time. Gabriel kept buying more shots….I tried to wake you up…"

"I was pissed off, and hurt. But then I felt so mean that I was pretending to be asleep. I've never done that before. I've never refused you like that." Alexandra bursts into tears.

"Lexi, it's okay. I got over it."

"But…you should care! You should care that I didn't want to have sex with you. You hinted at sex all day, and then you made it sound like you'd be home much sooner…. Why'd you chose your friends over me?"

"I'm sorry I stayed out so late, I really am. I wasn't even having that much fun, it just kind of kept going. You know? I didn't realize it was so late. But it's not that big a deal that you didn't want to have sex." Clyde puts his arms around Alexandra. Alexandra relishes being held, her hair being smoothed, like a child's; she kisses his warm, scratchy neck, breathing in his familiar morning, musky, masculine smell.

"Mummy!! Mummy's awake," Linus yells as he runs into the kitchen. Molly toddles behind him, but suddenly falls flat onto the tiled kitchen floor. Clyde instantly releases Alexandra and picks up Molly, kissing her chubby cheeks, "Are you okay, buttercup?" Molly coos in his arms, unfazed by her sudden fall. Linus runs back into the living room to get a CD.

"Let's dance!" he shouts.

Alexandra stands all alone in the middle of the kitchen. *But why didn't you come home sooner?*

"Play song four, Daddy," Linus says giving Clyde *The Lion King* CD. "Mummy, come!" The song comes on, and they all four start dancing. *Why did you choose your friends over me?* Alexandra twirls with Molly, Linus jumps around, and Clyde wiggles his butt to make the kids laugh. *You even told me to wait up.* Clyde struts over to Alexandra to take Molly. *Didn't you want to have sex?* "Mummy!" Linus puts his arms out to Alexandra, who picks him up; he wraps his legs around his mother and they spin and sing together, "Hakuna Matata! What a wonderful phrase/ Hakuna Matata! Ain't no passing craze/ It means no worries for the rest of your days/ It's our problem-free philosophy/ Hakuna Matata!"

Why'd you give up so easily?, Alexandra thinks, spinning Linus fast, holding on to him for dear life, so tightly that she doesn't have to look at Clyde, swaying with Molly and trying to meet her eyes.

Down Time

Harold Hoefle

Down Time

"The fucking fucker's fucked."

"Excuse me?"

"The tramline motor. It quit twenty minutes ago."

Grey light pressed against the window as talk stopped at other tables in the mess. I went quiet too because I feared asking the man a stupid question. Instead I watched him put his hardhat and styrofoam cup on my table, then wipe his brow with the sleeve of his coveralls. Grease smeared his forehead. Long, flat, black hair made his whole head seem oiled. Blinking sweat from his eyes, he looked half-human, half-engine-part.

"You're the new hire," he said, eyeing my silver earrings. "Security."

"I'm waiting for Bren O'Hearne."

The man scowled and ripped off part of his cup's lid.

"That prick stole my girl." The man pointed behind me. "Belly — that's her behind the counter."

I turned but couldn't see a woman. Though I remembered one.

"Is he still with her?" I said.

The man shook his head from left to right, and I watched hair swat his face.

"She even came crawling back to me, but *I* wouldn't take her. You need some pride in this hole."

He tore open three packets from the table bowl and dumped the sugar into his coffee. He muttered something.

"Down time," he said, louder. "We don't fix that motor by noon, they'll be sending men home for sure."

"Do they still get paid?"

"First five days. Don't know if that applies to you though." The man slurped his coffee. "Your boss might need you in case things get weird. Fights, B&Es, sabotage. Or he might just send you back to where you're from."

The man's mouth twitched at the sound of footsteps. After a glance behind him, he picked up his hardhat and left.

"Walter Schwende?" A tall man with blue eyes sat down. A moustache and sunburnt cheeks gave him a cowboyish look. His eyes travelled from my earrings to the rows of coveralled men, their heads bent and their forks moving up and down. A few men glanced our way.

"I bet Fratzie had some choice words for me."

"If you're Bren, one or two."

Bren shook his head. "That's the town of Clayton right there. I'll be glad to get out."

"You're leaving?"

"In about 356 hours — not that I'm counting." Bren spread his hands and tapped the table. "Guess you flew into Watson Lake last night. Where you from — Vancouver?"

"Toronto. Scarborough, actually." I picked at my cold eggs.

"An Upper Canadian," Bren said. He stuck out his hand. "Welcome."

The clamminess of his palm surprised me.

He was rubbing the crowned heart tattoo on his arm when a female voice ignited laughs nearby. The woman who'd served me walked towards us, trays stacked in her arms. Fratzie's stolen ex.

"How are ya, Belly?" Bren said.

"Better than most — as you know." She looked me over. "You're the new S/G."

I read the lettering on her baseball cap: *Sahara Marina*.

"I wear it for the subtle man," she winked, and walked off.

Bren thrust a thumb in her direction. "That woman can do things with six inches of cock that a monkey couldn't do with forty foot of rope."

I pushed aside my plate. Bren stared at the bread crusts and bacon fat.

"Any women here my age?" I asked, scanning the room. Beyond the window the grey light had thinned, revealing the shapes of trees and shingled buildings.

Bren looked at me. "Sprightly things are rare. So are single ladies. We've got seven. But you better be careful. Around here, there's a lot of scuffling for a honey. Just last week some hardhat shot a guy in the stomach for taking his girl."

"But did she willingly go with the guy?"

"That doesn't matter."

*

We walked along a gravel road that curved towards the town limits, and at the rec centre we met a crew sodding the front lawn. Bren introduced me to Keri, a native girl with short hair, a purple halter-top and a space between her front teeth. She stopped rolling out sections of grass to stare at me and smile.

As Bren and I neared the mill-site, large glossy ravens lifted and fell around us, their caws and thuffs seeming to deepen the creases in Bren's face. Pickup wheels rumbled and engines revved in the distance. An eighteen-wheel truck rattled past the security gate and towards the road out of town. The driver shouted Bren's name, then drew a hand across his neck. I looked at Bren but he glanced away, fixing his eyes on the smoke rising from a mill-site building, the white plumes twisting into a sky of washed-out blue.

A short man stood between the hut and the security gate. He looked like authority: the epauletted shirt and creased pants, the side-parted grey hair, the eyes brown and dull.

Bren spoke. "Ron Tenet, Walter Schwende. Our new S/G."

Ron raked his eyes over me. "You're a day late."

"In Vancouver they said to report for work on May 27th."

"I'll try to forget your first mistake, Mr. Schwende. But I'm wondering one thing — why here? You could get beat up back East just as easy."

Bren led me away after telling Ron we'd be touring the mill-site.

Clumps of pale green asbestos stuck to our boots as we walked between long buildings with ribbed roofs. When workers saw Bren, most looked away.

"Welcome to Pleasantville," he said.

"What makes Ron like that?"

Bren nudged me with an elbow. "Look around."

Lunch buckets in hand, men streamed out of buildings and pulled off their hardhats, some men flinging them onto the ground. At least two hundred workers converged on the security gate and the road to town. Down time; for now, work was over. No one looked our way, though I saw some empty stares and wet cheeks, heard men swear at the ground or each other. I turned to Bren. I didn't understand the grin on his face, the ends of his mouth tugged upward as if he couldn't control them.

*

After lunch a knock on my bunkhouse door startled me. I opened the door to Bren. He stood there in a plaid shirt with rolled-up sleeves, his right-hand dangling a six-pack of Kokanee. He gaped at my hair.

"I should've warned you."

I hadn't seen him since our tour of the mill-site. He'd dropped me off at the security hut, where Ron proceeded to overwhelm me: first with the reek of his aftershave lotion, then with details. He showed me how to write reports, man the gate, operate the walkie-talkie, use the time-clock and logbook. He stressed the need to check the backs of trucks for fresh kill, moose or caribou. Poachers hid them under tarps and blankets. And the poachers had to use the security gate because it blocked the sole access to a valley owned by the mine. I had to be especially cautious now: less work activity meant fewer people around, and poachers would feel bold. My job was to log all details of an encounter with a poacher and immediately notify Bren, the security-company adjutant. Ron added that I should never try to apprehend someone. Pushing up his sleeves, he held out forearms full of crooked scars. *Knife fights*, he said, *from the good old days*. Ron made me take out my earrings and then he sent me to Clayton's barber for a brush-cut. Now I looked like an extra on "Happy Days."

Bren surveyed the pants and books on my floor, levered the caps off two beers with his belt buckle and handed one over.

"Lube up before your first shift."

Someone passed by the window, grinding the gravel.

"Maybe one," I said. "I don't want Ron smelling booze on my breath."

Bren sat in the only chair and drank. "Listen, don't go thinking we're *all* assholes."

"Hey," I laughed, "I attract abuse."

"Maybe you do. But people here need enemies. As if letting a guy be different is wimpy, like you don't have a stance worth defending. And if you don't mind me saying, you seem like a real city-type. We're not used to seeing guys with their ears pierced three times."

I lifted my shoulders and dropped them; I didn't know what else to do.

"Bren, someone said you've worked in mines for thirty years. Twenty here. You must've seen a lot."

He held up his bottle. "A lot of these. And women even curvier."

He pulled a thick wad of bills from his pants pocket. After licking his fingertips, he made the money crack by rubbing each bill between his thumb and index finger. I saw browns and reds.

Constantly wetting his fingers, the money just inches from his face, Bren counted his wad three times. When he finished his last count, he held aside a hundred-dollar bill and looked at me. Then he stuffed all his money back in his pocket.

"Soon," he smiled, "I'll be smacking my cash down on some realtor's desk. 50 Gs. All for a tidy little place back in God's country." Bren leaned towards me. "But I'm still five grand away from peace-of-mind. From security." He coughed, a harsh rasping sound that seemed to stay in the room. "That, sir, is the only reason I'm still here. Get some new business and collect some old debts."

I heard the bunkhouse door open and close.

"How old is Keri?" I said.

Bren grinned. "Old enough. You know what they say — 'Fifteen'll get you twenty, but sixteen'll get you laid.'"

He looked at my face like he was trying to read it.

"She's a good girl though, that one. Plays on her school's baseball team. Don't think she's ever had a boyfriend but I wouldn't really know, there being about thirty-five years between us."

"Bren — " I paused "— I'm worried about what'll happen to me."

"You mean down time? Hey, they'll need security more than ever. You'll be fine. Just stick with your buddy Bren."

"But you're leaving."

"Got to." Bren coughed, wiped his mouth with his fingers. "Walter, look around. Behind almost everyone you see there's a broken marriage, a broken country, a crime, a drug or drinking problem. The North will let you hide and heal. At first." Bren drank.

"Then suddenly you've got money and only your old mistakes to spend it on. That's no fun. So you party, buy toys, buy whores in Whitehorse, take fancy trips, run up crazy debts on your credit card. You came to Clayton thinking you'd stay just long enough to kill some debt and tuck away some cash. Twenty years later you can't leave." Bren tipped back the rest of his beer. "That was *al*most my story, till I decided to turn things around." He patted his pocket.

"So you're going back to Newfoundland," I said. "Alone."

Smiling, Bren opened another beer. "A week or so trolling the George Street bars in St. John's, and I'll secure a lady willing to share my sheets." Bren drank. "Not a lot of options back home, and I'll be the man with money, a house, and endless charm and wit."

"All the charm and wit you learned here."

"Exactly."

Bren drained his second beer. He told me to meet him at the security gate at three o'clock, an hour away. When he left I lay on my bed and stared at the pine beams supporting the roof. One beam had graffiti on it, but I was too tired to get up and look. Too tired yet too nervous. I tried not to think about my first shift. And I wondered about Bren. Why would he expose so much of himself to someone he hardly knew? Maybe it was because we had no history — with me, he could start all over. I knew the strategy.

An hour into my first shift I sat in the security hut and, shielding my eyes from the sun, gazed at the electronic accident-prevention board across the road. Apparently the Warehouse had gone 3462 days without an "LTA" — a long-term accident, Bren explained. At the bottom of the board, flanked by orange double-triangles, glared a warning:

REMEMBER

SAFETY IS A STATE OF MIND

For the next two hours Bren leaned against the filing cabinet while I answered the phone, manned the gate, and recorded the license plates of eighteen vehicles in the logbook. Fratzie came through, nodding at me and throwing a slit-eyed look at Bren. I also met the tie-clad mine manager and mill superintendent. I didn't recognize their accents; Bren said they were South African. Later, when he was in the washroom I lifted the gate and had a talk with a diesel mechanic. He told me the mechanics were *givin' 'er*, taking the entire tramline motor apart.

I returned to the hut and found Bren outside, staring at the sky. He coughed. Without turning, he told me to take my supper break.

On my return I picked up the time clock and walked the mill-site. Near the end of my inspection a sudden rain drenched me. Twenty minutes later the sun came out, its glow turning everything orange: the mill-site buildings, the jack pines, the distant rec centre and mess, the jagged mountains that circled the town like sentinels. Soon the sun fell from sight.

Bren was still on supper break and I was alone at the gate when the red pickup pulled up, a dark tarp covering a large object in the back. The driver rolled down his window and said he was a mine-site engineer. He politely asked me to open the gate so he and his partner could get to the mess before they closed the kitchen.

"I have to check your back," I said.

"Just drills and a pile of tramline cable under that there tarp. Give us a break, buddy. We're starving."

I looked at the passenger's back and upturned collar.

I was about to go to the gate when I noticed two rifle-butts sticking out from a blanket behind the cab's seat.

"Sorry," I said to the driver. "I have to check every truck."

Beneath the tarp was the flank of a huge, brown-skinned animal.

The door slammed; the driver stood beside me. He'd brought a waft of booze. "12-pointer. We've been tracking this bull since dawn. C'mon bud, make your life easy. You don't want to write a report. Just do us a favour and lift the gate."

The passenger came around to my side of the truck. He wore mirror-sunglasses. Under the glare of the streetlamp, he looked like a small-time hood.

"Hey Skinny, where's Bren?"

I looked at his sunglasses, saw my oversized hardhat and green coveralls, then turned around and lifted the gate. The pickup sped off. In the hut, I recorded the license-plate number and the departure time in my log, but nothing else. When Bren returned I told him what I'd seen and he apologized, said I shouldn't have to be put on the spot like that. He checked the logbook and wrote down what he said was the poacher's name. Bren told me he'd talk to Ron. He

added that, under no circumstances whatsoever, should I tell anyone
what had happened — including Ron.

Something was obviously up, but I kept quiet. At 10:45 the night-
shift S/G arrived. As Bren and I walked under a starless sky back to
the town-site, he told me I'd done well. He'd reviewed my patrol
reports and the log. He said they were impressively detailed yet to-
the-point. I looked forward to a beer with him in our bunkhouse TV
room.

*

One night later, Keri showed up at my door. It was after midnight
and I'd just returned from a snack at the mess.

She stood in my room and looked at the floor. She wore a Good
Hope Lake baseball cap, jean jacket, and grey sweat pants stuffed
into construction boots. Her left arm cradled the town's house-
warming gift: a six-pack of Kokanee. She handed me a beer.

"I can't open it," I said.

She smiled slightly and bent down by the end of the bed. Lifting
up the carpet, she withdrew an opener.

Keri sat in the chair and I sat on the bed. I looked at her. I didn't
know what to think — or say. I just stared and drank my beer,
watching her drink hers. She didn't seem at all nervous. She sat there
like a guy, legs wide apart and feet flat on the floor.

Finally I said, "What grade are you in?"

"Going into twelve."

I thought to myself, okay, she's seventeen or eighteen. Hopefully
the latter.

"Are you *into* school?"

"I skip a lot." She downed the rest of her beer. She opened
another and passed me one, too.

I leaned forward. "You're not worried about failing?"

"They can't fail natives. People would call 'em racist. The
principal would lose his job."

I scratched my head.

"Hey," she said. She got up and stretched, her hands reaching towards the ceiling beams. "Do you do massages?"

On each of the next five nights Keri visited me, always around midnight. My room was at the end of the bunkhouse: she'd tap the corner of my window and I'd let her in the back door. We had to be quiet, which was easy in one way. She hardly spoke.

*

"Hear the rumour?"

It was a bright afternoon, my first day off after working six, and I was scuffling towards the town library when the truck stopped beside me. Its side-window framed the scruffy face of Fratzie, his eyes bulging as he waited for my response. He continued to wait.

It had happened four times: a pickup at the gate, Bren on supper break, and a driver telling me to not check his back. When one guy slipped me a white envelope and said give it to Bren, the obvious became even more so. Bren was making as much cash as possible before he went home, and I was his accomplice. Now I didn't know what to do. Unlike the other S/Gs, who seemed to have their own cliques, Bren had been kind to me since I arrived in Clayton. But maybe that was the point: he was just buying me off. Emotionally.

"What's the rumour?" I said to Fratzie.

He'd heard that the mine's superintendents had flown to Vancouver to see the owners and recommend that the mine be permanently shut down. World asbestos prices had plummeted and the owners had mining options in Mexico, where labour costs were a third of Clayton's.

Fratzie shook his head, greasy locks swishing against his cheeks. "The bigwigs don't give one runny shit about us. Twelve hundred jobs. All the families. And a lot of guys are way too old to get work elsewhere." He spat in the road. "I was just at the mine-site — we still can't find the problem. And starting today we don't get paid." Fratzie stared at me, his eyes bloodshot. "The world just wants to fuck you."

I nudged his tire with my shoe and a pickup cruised by, Steve Miller's "Big Ol' Jet Airliner" blasting into the air, a dog sitting upright in the cab's front seat. The driver stuck his hand out the window and gave Fratzie the finger. He, in turn, honked his horn, then smiled at me.

"So, shagged any of our women yet?"

I rested my arm on the cab's door. "Keri Macey."

Fratzie peered at my face. "Where'd you do her? The firebreak?"

"She comes to my room."

Looking over my shoulder, he whispered: "Home delivery."

"Every night."

Fratzie put the truck in gear and drove off towards his trailer at the end of town.

*

On my next shift, I was writing up my patrol report in the security hut when Bren called me outside.

"Check out the nightlife."

For once the sky wasn't clouded over. Streaks of green and yellow light zigzagged in a sky speckled by stars.

I went with Bren back into the hut and plugged in the kettle. He was examining the logbook when I spoke.

"What about the poaching, Bren?"

I had to say his name again before he turned.

"Walter, I know what's in your head. You see me breaking company rules. Lying. Listen, you've been here, what — a week? You're nowhere near figuring this place out."

The kettle whistled and Bren made us coffee. My job.

"But why poaching?" I said. "If the mine's higher-ups find out, won't they think we're a slack outfit and fire *all* of us? Eight guys would lose jobs because of you. Eight guys with the kinds of debts you've told me about."

Bren came up to me, his hands loose at his sides. He was smiling. "Tell me something, buddy. When Keri's lying on her stomach and you're doin' her from behind, do you notice how the bear-tattoo on her left shoulder seems alive?"

Bren folded his arms across his chest and looked out at the accident-prevention sign.

The phone rang. A jubilant mine-manager told me the tramline motor was fixed — the mechanics spotted a sheared piece of metal and replaced it. When I told Bren, he swore and struck out at the desk, knocking his coffee all over my report. On our walk back to the mess he asked me if I'd rat on him. I said no, but was glad the darkness hid the look on my face. In the mess he asked me again.

*

The firebreak cut a rocky swath through the jack pines around the town-site, creating a jump supposedly too wide for flames to leap. Ever since a fellow S/G showed me this secluded path, and especially the high point from which you could view the mountains and mill-site, the tailings pile and town-site, I'd often come up here with my hand-sized cassette player and a Billy Bragg tape. Now I walked on the small rocks with Keri. Our first outing, albeit one hidden from public view. S/Gs, according to Ron Tenet, shouldn't fraternize with the townspeople.

It was Saturday, just after lunch, and my shift started at 3. I was surprised when Keri agreed to meet me. She'd said yes at 1 this morning.

So we walked. And I swatted mosquitoes, wondering whether to ask my questions.

She wore a pink tanktop and her baseball cap, along with jeans and a pair of Greb Kodiaks. Apart from a soft "hi" when we met, she hadn't spoken. We just moved on, picking our steps carefully. The firebreak was mostly quiet: the trees seemed empty of ravens and chipmunks, and an electric saw buzzed in the town-site. Otherwise, just the sound of our boots hitting the rocks.

"You drive a Cat?" Keri said.

"A car and a van, but that's it." I didn't think she knew how to operate a backhoe, and I didn't understand why she'd asked the question.

"My dad drives a flatbed truck," she said, and palmed the sweat off her forehead. "He makes $175 a day. Pretty awesome, eh?"

I nodded. "You got your driver's license?"

"Next year. But sometimes my brother lets me drive his truck, like when we go four-wheeling up in the mountains. That way he can ride shotgun and drink."

We were on the rise. The tailings pile rose in the distance, a fifty-metre-high mound of ore detritus, full of flaky light-green stuff that sure looked like asbestos.

"We end up breathing that," I said.

"We're breathing it right now," said Keri. "We'll all die soon. Easterners first."

I laughed.

"Hey," I said, "do you talk much to Bren?"

She turned her back and began to walk in the direction we'd come from. I caught up to her, and was ready to say something when she turned and looked at me.

"I've seen him french a dog. He's disgusting."

We went back to the firebreak's start, and Keri didn't say a word. Before we went our separate ways, I stopped and took in her smooth face, her slouch.

"Hey," she said. "I want to tell you a joke."

"Shoot."

"I forget," she said, and walked away.

A few hours later, on my afternoon shift, I watched Bren leave the hut for supper. He swung his hardhat back and forth as he walked. I still didn't know how he'd heard about Keri. No way Fratzie would've told him. Did Bren arrange for Keri to see me? That was hard to believe, given the firebreak talk her and I just had. I couldn't even believe that she'd told him. On our walk she was the most talkative I'd seen, but in my room she hardly ever talked, despite the fact that we slept together every night. She didn't like questions. Whenever I asked about her family, her friends, the town itself, she just shrugged and took my hand, placing it where she wished. Keri came to see me but I was always the guest, being taken to rooms she wanted me to visit.

Loud honking announced the arrival of the fuel truck. The driver was my age. He had long sideburns and a diamond stud in each ear. He wore oil-splattered jeans and he reeked of gasoline. Tonight Fratzie sat with him in the cab.

"Wally boy," smiled the driver. "I hear your pujoginator's on night shift."

"Night wiggle," smirked Fratzie.

I laughed. People here spoke a different language.

"That Keri Macey," said the driver, "she goes like a skidoo without a kill switch."

Fratzie punched him in the shoulder. I raised the gate and they drove off, coughing exhaust behind them. That and their laughter hung in the air, along with their talk. I kicked the base of the gate, denting it with my steel-toed boot.

I walked back to town after my shift and took little notice of the green and yellow lights zipping across the sky. I skipped my usual mess snack and went straight to my room. I tried to read but couldn't last beyond a paragraph. As I waited for Keri, all I could think about was her slow, lazy movements — from door to chair to bed — and the smell of her sweat. But now I wondered whether it was just *her* sweat. And that night, for the first time in eight, she didn't show up. At five a.m. I was still lying awake on my bed, glancing every few minutes at the red-and-black face of my clock radio. At one point I stood up and read the graffiti scribbled on the ceiling-beam, presumably put there by a former S/G, maybe someone who had also known about the beer opener under the carpet.

It doesn't kill you.

It doesn't make you stronger.

It's a waste of time.

*

Saturday morning. Overcast. Ravens hopped on the roofs as I walked to the store in search of a *Globe and Mail*.

Today was Bren's last day in Clayton; tomorrow morning he'd be taking a bus to Watson Lake. And Keri — she hadn't come to my room in five nights.

I waited for a pickup to pass me on the gravel road. The truck's stereo blared "Sweet Home Alabama" and the driver touched his baseball cap when he saw me. I went through the glass doors of the store, picked up a three-day-old *Globe* and lined up at the checkout counter behind a woman in a familiar jacket. She was putting groceries on the conveyor belt.

"Keri."

She didn't flinch.

"Five bucks even," said the cashier, lank hair falling over the front of her sweatshirt. She frowned at me and I wanted to scream.

I moved closer to Keri as she shoved her groceries in a bag.

"Keri," I said.

She turned around. I looked at the white T-shirt beneath her jacket, at her grey eyes.

"Sir, that'll be one dollar for *The Globe*."

I watched Keri's back as she walked out of the store. I paid the cashier and went to the mess, stopping once to bite my fingertips.

At the end of the long room, his back against the wall, Fratzie sat alone. He waved me over. I didn't see Bren. He was likely collecting envelopes, hustling from trailer to house to bunkhouse.

Fratzie's cheeks were pouched with food and he just nodded when I sat down with my tray. He wiped gravy and bits of steak off his plate with a slice of bread, moving it in ever-smaller circles until the plate was spotless. He ate the bread and asked if I was going to The Spill — Clayton's bar — for Bren's going-away party.

"Ron said S/Gs shouldn't fraternize in the bar."

Fratzie burped. "Come tonight. It'll give you an edge." He winked. "You show up where you're not expected, people need time to react. When they know you're comin' they get their ammo all set, all ready to plug you."

I nodded and then ate while he drank his coffee and got a refill. When he sat back down I thought, to hell with it.

"Fratzie, do you know about Bren's poaching?"

"Of course."

"I thought you hated him."

Fratzie put down his cup. "What are you trying to do?" He shook his head. "One thing you don't do here is rat. Even if you rat on an asshole, people just peg you for a rat." Fratzie drained his cup. "Walter, people here run rats out of town, or stomp them till blood comes out their ears."

I leaned over the table and hissed: "Then why does everyone here keep telling *me* stuff? Including you?"

He pushed his face close to mine.

"Around here, blabbing's like breathing. That's why most people are so messed up. They come here messed up, then they get worse." Fratzie stood. "So almost everyone's a rat, but they're all different sizes. And you can't see the smart ones."

I walked back to the bunkhouse to change into my coveralls. The sun laid down its heat and I was making the only noise around. The ravens listened.

*

Just before Bren took his supper-break, he handed me a coffee and said: "I'm about to kill him. The bastard trailing me my whole time here."

I was suddenly afraid — for Fratzie.

Bren pulled out his wad of bills and performed his finger-lick ritual.

"Who's your enemy?" I said.

He smiled, put on his hardhat. At the door he paused but didn't turn. "Regret."

My shift was uneventful. No poachers, no white envelopes. At 11 p.m. Bren didn't want to walk back to the mess together, but he promised to meet me later at The Spill. He had to talk to the night-shift S/G.

In my room I listened to pickup doors slam, one after another. Men and women were arriving at the bar after short drives from their homes, trailers, bunkhouse digs. I heard voices and laughter: the bar was filling up. People were primed to party, and all I could do was lie in my bed and wonder whether Keri would be there. Impossible.

I put on my earrings and Doc Marten boots.

When I entered The Spill, smoke made me cough. I edged past a dance floor surrounded by clumps of men clutching drinks, and at the bar I found a banner draped under the counter: A SHOTGUN PATROLS THIS BAR ONE NIGHT A WEEK. YOU GUESS WHICH NIGHT.

I bought a beer and stood against a wall, at the edge of shouts, clinking bottles and power-chord rock. I stared at the heads of unknown men and women, some covered by baseball caps and cowboy hats. After four beers I was still alone, elbows poking me as talk of the mine wafted my way. I looked at the door and wondered about Bren. But he never showed up, nor did I see anyone else I knew. I drank until last call.

As I was squeezing past the puddled tables on my way out, a hand fell on my shoulder. A tall man slipped a beer into my hand. He was a poacher.

"You on afternoons next week?"

"Yes."

"Should I give *you* the envelope?"

I looked at him. Then I shook my head.

The man grabbed the front of my shirt. "What do I do now?" he said, his mouth hanging open. I said nothing and finally he let go and drifted away, back into the groups of people splayed out beside their tables.

I went after him. When I pulled hard on his shoulder he turned around, his fist cocked.

I spoke into his right ear. "I'll take it."

I walked back to the bunkhouse in the dark. Six cans of Kokanee beer were taped to my door and behind them was a thank-you note from Bren. I went down to his room and found it empty. I tried our TV room. A new poster announced a town meeting next Friday in the rec centre. The mine's owners wanted to talk to workers and their families. Someone with a black marker had written *Ghost Town* across the poster's bottom. Someone else, in a red, smaller script, had scrawled *Get Out Now*.

Notes on Contributors

Tom Abray grew up in a pink farmhouse near Strathroy, Ontario. He began writing his first novel, a Hardy Boys rip-off, in grade 5, but hit a wall after three pages. After high school he moved to Montréal and after obtaining his M.A. he joined the John Abbott College English department. His short stories and poems have appeared in journals like *Prairie Fire*, *Fiddlehead*, and most recently *Descant*. His novella, *Pollen*, and novel, *Love Traffic,* are available at lulu.com.

Zsolt Alapi teaches in the English Department of Marianopolis College. His poetry and fiction has appeared in various venues in Canada, the U.S., and the UK. He is the former editor of the literary magazine, *Atropos*, and the editor of *Writing at the Edge: Fiction that Takes Risks*. Forthcoming is a chapbook from Black Bile Press and a collection of stories entitled *The Art of Hiding in Trees*. He is the editor and publisher of Siren Song Publishing.

Tanya Bellehumeur-Allatt teaches in the English Department at Champlain Regional College, in Lennoxville. Her poetry has been published in *Room, Crux*, and in *Taproot II* and *III,* anthologies of Eastern Townships writing. She has also been shortlisted for *Event*'s Creative Non-Fiction writing competition. Tanya lives in North Hatley with her husband and four young children.

Philip Dann was born in Saint John, New Brunswick on the same day that the Loch Lomond Mall burned down. His poetry has appeared in *Vox*, a literary journal from the University of New Brunswick in Saint John, and he credits the underground Arts scene of that foggy city for fostering his creative energy. He has been teaching English at Marianopolis College for five years.

Jill Goldberg is a Montréal ex-pat currently living in Vancouver. While in Montréal, she taught English Literature at Vanier and Marianopolis College, and most recently has been teaching in Vancouver at Langara College. Jill is also a shiatsu practitioner, a former dancer/choreographer and has had writing and photography in publications including *Matrix Magazine* and *The Dance Current*.

Mara Gutmanis Grey was born in Latvia, grew up in Argentina, lived in Morocco and England, and travelled elsewhere. She teaches poetry, Latin American and Afro-American Literature at Dawson College and on occasion at Concordia University. She has written poems and stories but has rarely published, choosing to work on a Ph.D thesis instead on Jazz and Modern American poetry.

Sheryl Halpern was born in Montréal, Québec, and allowed herself to be brought up there in spite of the weather. She graduated from Skidmore College with a B.A. in English Literature, realized that she couldn't get a good job, went back and got an M.A. in English Literature from Queen's University, and realized that she still couldn't get a good job. She then got her Ph.D. in études anglaises from the Université de Montréal and is now a full-time college professor at Dawson College. She has published poetry in such magazines as *Quarry* and *New Quarterly*, has written articles for *The Montreal Gazette*, and reviews for *Books in Canada* and *Canadian Literature*.

Harold Hoefle teaches in the English Department of John Abbott College. His fiction and non-fiction have appeared in many anthologies and journals, including *The Antigonish Review*, *Grain*, and *The Windsor Review*. Black Bile Press has published his chapbook *Spray Job*. His story "Down Time" first appeared in *Exile*. In September, Oberon Press will publish his novel in stories, *The Mountain Clinic*.

Andrew McCambridge is a Montréal-based English teacher with over eight years experience at the post-secondary level. A former freelance journalist and business writer, Andrew has been teaching courses in mythology and Canadian fiction at Marianopolis College since 2006. "The Act" is his first foray into creative writing.

Greta Hofmann Nemiroff has been teaching in the CEGEP system since 1970 and is currently the Coordinator of the Creative Arts, Literature and Languages Program at Dawson College where she teaches English and Humanities at the New School. She has written articles and edited and written books related to Women's Studies and education. Her short stories have been published in anthologies and journals in Canada and the US.

Monique Polak has been teaching English and Humanities at Marianopolis College since 1985. She is the author of eight novels for young adults. Her next novel, *What World Is Left*, will be released by Orca Book Publishers in fall 2008. Monique is a frequent contributor to *The Montreal Gazette* and to Canwest publications across the country. Her work has also appeared in *The Globe and Mail*, *Newsday* and *Maclean's Magazine*.

Helen Siourbas teaches English at Champlain College St. Lambert, where she was once a Cegep student. She enjoys acquainting her students with the power of fantasy literature and of proper academic tone. She earned an M.A. in English Literature and a B.A. in Creative Writing from Concordia University, and has had fiction, poetry, creative non-fiction, and literary criticism published in various venues. Currently, she is writing reams of poetry, giving purpose to her fountain pen.

Lawrence L. Szigeti is a critic, writer, broadcaster, and life-long academic. He has appeared on the BBC, HATV, and TV2, while his criticism has been featured in *Jump Magazine*, *Lettre Internationale*, *Balkon*, *Helikon*, and *aea*. His latest interest is the exploration through literary means the intersection of physical and imagination-driven memory, which he calls "memofiction" (*And Then There Was Light*, 2002). Having taught at the university level in the U.S., Hungary, Manitoba, and Québec, he currently teaches English at Collège Jean-de-Brébeuf and John Abbott College. He is also the founding editor-in-chief of *aea*, a new Montréal-based initiative to create a venue for multicultural issues and writing.

Anushree Varma has taught at the Cegep du Vieux Montréal and Marianopolis College. In addition to writing fiction, she is also a painter and graphic artist who has taught many workshops in the Montréal area and abroad on forms of creative expression.

Sabine Walser teaches in the English Department at Marianopolis College. She has written articles for *Montreal Families*, CBC radio, and most recently has published a story in Siren Song's *Wrtiting at the Edge*.

Barry Webster has published fiction in both English and French. He was written for a wide variety of publications including *The Washington Post, The Globe and Mail, The Montreal Gazette* and *Virages*. His short fiction has been shortlisted for the *National Magazine Award* and the *CBC-Québec Prize*. His first book, *The Sound of All Flesh* was a finalist for the *Hugh MacLennan Prize* and won the *ReLit Award* for best collection of short fiction published by a Canadian press in 2005. He teaches at Marianopolis College.